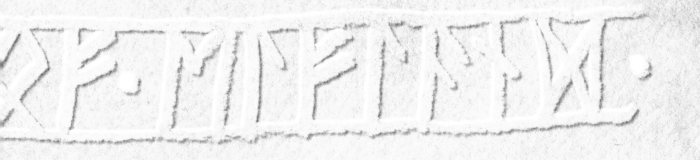

THE RUNES OF
ELFLAND

BRIAN FROUD AND ARI BERK

HARRY N. ABRAMS, INC., PUBLISHERS
NEW YORK

FOR
WENDY AND TOBY
&
KRISTEN AND ROBIN

Our particular thanks to our editors at Abrams, and to Robert Gould for his
friendship and vigilance, Tracy Ford for wordsmithing, Stacy Burnette for runes of
the road, William Spytma for northern lore, the company of Hawkwood for
midwinter rune-play, and our families for every good thing.

Art Copyright © 2003 Brian Froud
Text Copyright © 2003 Ari Berk

Designed by Emil Dacanay for Wherefore Art?

Library of Congress Cataloging-in-Publication Data
Froud, Brian
    [Runes of Elfland]
    The Runes of Elfland by Brian Froud and Ari Berk
    p. cm.
    ISBN 081094612-2
    1. Elves. 2. Runes. I. Berk, Ari. II. Title

GR540.F76 2003
398.2-dc21

Rune Artifacts by Jason Hancox
Photography by Brian Froud

™ World of Froud
Published in 2003 by Harry N. Abrams, Incorporated, New York

Printed and bound in Hong Kong

The text of this book was composed in Charlemagne, Garamond and Linoscript.

10 9 8 7 6 5 4 3 2 1
First Printing

Harry N. Abrams, Inc.
100 Fifth Avenue
New York, N.Y. 10011
www.abramsbooks.com

Abrams is a subsidiary of
 LA MARTINIÈRE
G R O U P E

Visit the Official Froud Faeries Website
www.WorldofFroud.com

A World of Froud/Imaginosis Book
www.imaginosis.com

CONTENTS

THE PAINTINGS AND STORIES

FOREWORD

When I was small and the trees were tall I spent my time in their company. I loved to climb high up into their leafy crowns: my favorite tree was the birch. I would climb as high as I could before my weight would bend the slender trunk down to the ground and I would be safely deposited on the earth. As I let go, the tree swooshed upwards, showering leaves over me. It was only recently, just before he died, that my father confided in me that he too, as a child, had climbed the "birch benders". At that moment we were not father and son but two small boys forever held close in fellowship.

Runes have always been a part of the fabric of my art. When I looked at a tree or a rock and images of faeries and trolls appeared, often there were accompanying runes. They were a secret code always holding a message albeit sometimes rather whimsical in content. But gradually I wondered what they really wanted to say. Their straight-lined forms have a power and urgency—no languid, meandering curves for them—only purposeful directness. I was intrigued by their ability to hold such vitality in their ancient patterns.

Runes come from a time when the world was still perceived as a magical place—when people felt connected to elves and dwarves, giants and dragons, when the tales they told of them were not received as fiction, but as history and the recounting of everyday events. Runes were incised on swords, helmets, sacred objects, stones, fragments of wood as- dedications of hope and desire, power and healing—always providing a connection to another hidden world of spiritual beings, the precise meanings of the angular sigils, or signs, never quite giving up all their deep secrets, always retaining their strange power. What meaning could these ancient forms have that spontaneously appeared in my art? When I looked around me their shapes seemed to be hidden in the crossed branches of trees, in the twisted roots; even my jumbled pencils appeared to insist there was a story to tell.

It was Ralph Blum, whose book of runes is one of the wisest books I have ever read, who encouraged me to paint pictures specifically about runes—to allow them to step from the background into the center stage. I looked at their shapes, and images came to mind; then I painted for months. I was astonished at how singular they all were—some quaint, some quirky, others bright and beautiful. Together they constituted a journey into deepest Faery, where I met so many different creatures on the way, all with their own stories to impart. Years passed and the paintings waited patiently in a corner of my studio, waiting for a storyteller to tell their tales. And so, once upon a time, in a land that is not my land, I met such a storyteller.

Ari Berk was a speaker at a Fairy Conference held at the Omega Center in New York State. The Omega Center is a beautiful and spiritual place; it is also strictly vegetarian. I somehow knew Ari was a kindred spirit, as we drove, lost in runic, zigzag patterns through the countryside on a quest, desperately seeking the holy grail, as it appeared to us that day:

pastrami sandwiches! As we shaped our journey and ate our pastrami, I realized that Ari not only had a deep knowledge of all things ancient and arcane; he also held in perfect harmony his heart and head. He was, in short, the perfect guide to unravel the elven runes. What a joy it has been to be in the safe company of Mr. Berk!

Mr. Berk's words ebb and flow with mystery and meaning. Words, often aloof and distant to me, are his friends. Images are my vocabulary, but I knew a foreword needed words, so I sought them in my local landscape.

High on the moors I found myself in a place called Grimspound, at the remains of a Bronze Age settlement. Here a story came to mind, of Odin, the Norse god who, by pain and sacrifice gained the runes and so was gifted with the power of wisdom and poetry. As I stood pondering this, I realized that Grim is another name for Odin himself. So, here in this ancient enclosure named after the lord of the runes, the blustering wind reminded me that the name Odin is thought to derive from the word for "wind," or "spirit." He certainly represents the wilder aspects of nature found in this landscape. He is still said to ride across the moor, leading his wild hunt. His spectral hounds are kenneled at nearby rocky Hound Tor. And the "craeking" of a raven, Odin's totem bird, is a sharp reminder that, even in the twenty-first century, runes and their stories can still powerfully connect us to our own landscapes, both inner and outer.

When I, the man, say hello to I, the boy, and when I climb those birch trees of long ago, I can tell him what I did not know then; that shamans climbed birch trees in their trances to gain access to inner worlds. That as he sits in the delicate branches, listening to the whispering leaves, he is being initiated into Faery. I can tell him that the runes were born from twigs, and that when I look at a rune I see twig-like forms that are a direct communication with Faery. I see potent patterns that evoke the wisdom of nature and inspire a deeper knowledge of ourselves and our relationship to our world. I can pass on the knowledge that in rune-lore, the birch is the tree of beginnings and my Beginnings, that my destiny was shaped by the boy in a birch tree.

Long ago in Wales, young girls would give a birch twig to their suitors as a sign that they could begin their courtship. I give you now a birch twig so that you may begin your adventure. Let the runes tell their tales!

Brian Froud
Chagford, Devon, England
October 2002

5

PREFACE

This book began with a question.

Brian and I, each in our own time, stood before the runes as artists, and both asked the same thing of them: "What are you hiding, then?" We wanted to know what stories stood behind the ancient letters. We wanted to see where those stories might take us. We wanted to find the hidden lands within the lore. Brian painted. I wrote. This book is our answer to that question, our record of what we found within the runes.

My work with the runes continues to be a process of seeing, listening and remembering. I remember walking far into a redwood forest and emerging from the canopy at a place where driftwood logs were polished like bones and stacked up by the sea. I remember listening to wind move across the mouth of a cave and trying to interpret its language. I remember all the lands I've seen and walked, and the secrets they held, kept in moss and hidden under stone. I remember all the tales I've ever been told or read. And I've begun to recall some of the ideas I formed as a child about the power of letters.

When I was young, I loved the mysterious letters of ancient cultures and was particularly fascinated by the hieroglyphs of Egypt. I remember learning that hieroglyphs of certain animals, like lions, would sometimes be drawn without their heads for fear that the glyph-animal might come to life, springing suddenly from the wall upon which it was inscribed. I was deeply intrigued by the belief that letters or words might leap from the page and take on lives of their own. What if such a thing were possible? And if it could happen with Egyptian hieroglyphs, why not with any alphabet, in any land, at any time? As my interest in letters grew, I learned of runes and saw immediately with a child's eye that their shapes were the shapes of branches. I started to believe, and still do believe, that all the pieces of the natural world are a kind of living alphabet, each with a tale to tell, and that if you look at the land in the right manner, there are stories to be read in the way leaves fall upon the ground, in the patterns of bird flight, in the shadows of clouds moving across the moor.

This, then, is a living book.

You may read the Rune for Beginnings today, but what will that Rune mean to you twenty years from now?

After you plant a birch tree?

After you learn that crowns of birch were worn ceremonially by ancient people to signify the end of one life and the beginning of another?

After you walk to the birch wood?

After you turn the page?

INTRODUCTION:
The ABCs of the Runes of Elfland

A single word can be a world and every letter a land.

A rune drawn upon the ground can have curious consequences, might invite adventure, may open ancient doors. Here are the Runes of Elfland. Here are songs of the shining lands. Here are signs of crossing and threshold. Here are stories of fate and illumination.

Chant the charm, tell the tale, and step across. . .

Runes and the Language of Imagination

You hold a book of keys and crossroads, a living map to the gates of Elfland. A "map," because all art—written and painted—is a kind of guide, leading us to see the world in a new way. "Living," because when you read these charms and stories aloud, you are breathing life into these pages, awakening the enchanted world around you.

But what are runes?

Most often when people refer to runes, they are speaking of letters whose development, some think, began in the second or third century in northern Europe as adaptations of the Roman or Greek alphabet. But even this theory is contested. The forms of these letters are certainly evocative of (if not partially based on) the natural forms found in the forests of ancient Europe. So the shapes of these letters draw our minds close to the first forest of the world, and move our imaginations nearer to a time when the patterns of the land could be depicted creatively as signs and symbols, when letters might stand for many things: a sound, an embodiment of place, a spell, a fate.

The word "rune" originates in words meaning "secret," but "rune" has also come to mean "a poem, charm, or spell." *Runar* (from the Norse) means "a magical sign," and *runa*, (from Old German) is "to whisper a secret." "Hidden," "magic," whispers," all words long associated with Faery, the secret country. So when we talk of runes, we are speaking of objects that have multiple meanings, letters both worldly and otherworldly in origin and aspect. Their "secrets" may reside not so much in hidden meanings (though runes have many of these), but in ways of seeing the world. In this sense, each single rune creates layers of phonetics, poetry, and power built up over time. Runes are intended to endure. They record things that must be remembered or heeded. Runes are letters and words that must not be lost or wasted. They embody and express essential knowledge.

Who has not listened to hear the secret stories of the land whisper from ruins or forests, or from the pages of ancient texts? Whose soul has not stirred to this music of the past? Such subtle strains tell us the past is not a distant dead thing, but exists all around us, all the time.

Faery stories exist in just this way, by being at once both "here-and-there." Both language and Elfland are borderlands where the past and present conjoin. Because of this, faery stories are always current, no matter how strange they may seem, so long as we are able to see ourselves as parts of an ongoing dialogue between this world and the Other. In the same way, runes provide opportunities for conversing with the land, and its enchanted denizens.

More generally, runes represent lore—the preservation in symbol and memory of all that that is wondrous, powerful, inspiring, and wise. If we truly wish to understand the transformational power of the runes, we must travel the paths of tradition into Elfland, the stronghold of myth, magic, and imagination. The key to that land resides—as it always has—in the act of storytelling.

Even as children we know that letters are magic, the gateways to new stories and new ways of seeing the world. When we make our first tentative marks upon paper, we begin to understand the creative power inherent in letters and images. Runes help us to rediscover that magic. These rune paintings and stories belong to the ground and contain something of the past and present simultaneously. We can stand on a plot of earth that may also have been stood upon by people for many thousands of years and may contain traces of those ancient times, hidden just below the surface in the stories we continue to tell. Runes reflect the many ages and peoples that have used them, while also existing here and now, in the very moment of your recognition of them. Listen to the land. Look for signs. Watch the shapes of nature, the branches, the stones, their shadows. Here are the beginnings of tales waiting to be told.

Origins—
The Faery Alphabet of Branches

Early letters may still be seen in the lands of the north, marked by giants upon the stones. These are ancient, to be sure. But even before such signs were carved, words were read by wise elves within the arterial patterns on leaves, forms of angled branches, and the interlacing shadows on the forest floor.

Within the ancient and secret annals of Elfland are tales of the origin of letters, of how alphabets were found and shaped from natural forms. Over time, elvish letters found their way into human hands, becoming touchstones for mortal memory. First and most often they were used by mortals to legally recognize the names of landowners, make maps of empires, and further the petty needs of human commerce. But when used to record myth and hearth tale, prayer and song, the letters retained something of their original elvish purpose and might still remind the wise eye of the sacredness inherent in simple, living things. If we look carefully at the growing world around us we shall see that these runes are still there in the land's living shapes, awaiting our discovery.

The sacredness of letters is largely forgotten in modern times because our contemporary alphabets have become abstract. The letters of the Roman alphabet are no longer directly connected either to symbolic meanings or to forms of the land. But with runes, we may again experience the power and poetry of a magical alphabet. Each letter has a sound, but also a story, that relates to a particular mythic world. These living letters and images are still full of portent and possibility: verdant lullabies, maps of the secret goblin provinces sprawling invisibly below the ground, solsticial sonnets, berry songs, root wisdom, elvish prayers and puns, charms, alphabets, or the secret names that fade from our memories as we enter this world.

The oldest human lore still hints of this pre-mortal time, when primal powers blossomed in the growing forms of the land. Oak, ash, and thorn are not only trees, but also creatures, images, symbols, shapes, sounds, particular motions of objects moved by winds, and, as the ancient carvings attest, even gods. The sounds of their names, the shapes of their leaves and branches are all evocations, shards of a sacred faery language that may even now be learned. Our own history is rooted in the fertile ground of Faery, for eventually we came to live beneath the shelter of trees, building nations from and beneath the boughs. We still dream surrounded by the timbered bodies of ancient gods; through the runes and the telling of their tales, we may awaken them from their slumber.

Runes as Faery Stories

Through the runes, we will see Elfland as an entire world, or a series of connected and intersecting sensual worlds inhabited by powerful beings, each world with its own natural laws, each with its own kind of language. And of course, each part of Faery has its own preferred manner of storytelling, reflecting some great age of the world or curious otherworldly influence, or just the renowned vagaries of elvish fashion.

Traditionally, these otherworldly people are referred to as "faeries," or a "faery" if you are only referring to one. Just to confuse matters, they insist that their own country is called "Faery" as well (and it is always capitalized), but we may also call it Elfland, an ancient and well-respected word indeed. If you truly wish to be accepted into the inner circle of Elfland, you will always remember that the word "faery," in all its guises should be pronounced with three syllables (*fay-er-ree*), and never only two.

Faery languages may be manifested in many ways. Gesture, motion, artistry can all derive from the runes and reflect faery forms of knowledge. Such forms invite our interaction and creative experimentation. Tell the stories, yes, but also draw them, paint them, make the signs with your hands, or with branches, or form them with your body.

Even today, among clever folk, faery stories are still vital and necessary, aspects of ancient living traditions, because they do far more than merely entertain. They delineate boundaries between this world and the Other, they express important rules of conduct, they identify safe pathways through the tangled forests of our lives. They keep us well warned and out of trouble. They are vessels of our collective wisdom, recorded, treasured, and handed down from times past.

The power of faery stories resides in their ambiguity. Faery stories are often anonymous tellings, which insures that they never belong completely to one period. They express timeless narratives handed down through oral tradition. They may adapt themselves to any moment, any fashion, any person. This is because they are associated more with landscape and mythic memory than with historical periods (though they have stealthily entered the historical record as well). Such stories, so long as they are told, continue to express the particular nature of a given land: the *genius loci*, the "intelligence of place." It is through faery stories that we may come to understand our connection to the land and its elemental and spiritual heart.

Like the paintings before you, the runes themselves are not merely individual letters but composite creations, built from visions, songs, riddles, spells, charms, and legends; a host of often subtle, always compelling concepts bound together in a single expressive form. A line becomes a noble tree trunk; a curve, the spread of branching antlers. Each painting is both an emblem of a unique, living world and the key to that world. Each of these runic tales and its faery guardian has something to tell us, some perspective to impart, some new landscape to open to our senses.

Landscape and Storytelling

Every myth, legend, or faery story ever told is, at least in part, about a human relationship with the land. At places on the land where people encounter the wondrous, we will often find a story left behind to commemorate the event. As both letters and stories, runes are often associated with these locations, marking them for future generations, waiting for the right storyteller to come along. Through our experiences with these faery stories, it becomes immediately clear that we are talking about worlds that are familiar and strange at the same time. Such is the nature of Elfland: it is not somewhere else, but just there, beyond the next hill, within the dark wood, always at the edge of the familiar, but never entirely separated from it.

Like magic itself, Elfland is associative. So any landscape may provide a way in if its story is known and spoken. The scrub land at the end of your street has its roots in ancient forests; parks where we now play may border the meadowlands of old; any substantial boulder in a farmer's field may speak of barrows, and henge circles; many of our cities echo the angles and walls of ancient labyrinths, and it takes little more than our acknowledgment of this to activate those hallowed associations, making them available to our imagination. Think of places you know, landscapes in your memory—abandoned cemeteries, greening ruins and crumbling walls; somber, stately houses; deep and darkening woods; overgrown gardens; a patch of waste ground within your town; even an empty city alleyway that gives you pause; places where you feel a bit unsettled or become filled with awe and wonder. These are the places where we are inspired to speak a quiet prayer, to draw or write, to dance and sing among the stones, to hide, or to bravely walk alone. Whether you find yourself in marsh or fen, in woodland or meadow, in garden or ruin, in city or country, know that any place may provide a door to Elfland if the right runes are known, if the right stories are spoken.

Imagine speaking the charm and reading these stories: Your words go out into the world. The old places are awakened. Now rising about you are the ghosts of ancient trees, twisted low, worn by the weight of time. Here are standing stones, a broken wall. Their quiet gives the place a sense of breadth and every sound, from footfall to the distant bird call, sinks deep into the mossy ground and is held within. From the edge-wood, the Faery Guardian emerges to join you for the telling of its tale.

As your voice rises and falls like the land, you will come to stand between the worlds, between the present and the past in the living moment of the tale's telling. Through storytelling, we ask the mythic world to stir and acknowledge us. Beyond the sound of our own voices, we may hear the horns of Elfland and in that way know that the gates of Faery are close at hand.

Doors and Boundaries of Elfland

Storytelling brings us close to Elfland, but what do its doors look like? How will you know when you are at the threshold of the Otherworld? Well, such doors are all around us, all the time (at your fingertips, even now), though they are not always obvious. The Otherworld is a flickering presence, subtly intersecting our own familiar landscapes.

Traditionally, the doors to the Otherworld are sought in lonely places—forests, wastes, and islands—but can be found anywhere individuals closely connect with communal, ancestral landscapes. Indeed, if bestowed with runic images, even the pages of a book may provide a door. We can also enter Elfland by imaginatively entering the story itself, by seeing ourselves as an integral part of the plot. We *become* the characters of the faery stories every time we tell them with open hearts and minds.

Throughout the ages, particular kinds of stories and special images seem to emerge repeatedly to indicate when Faery is close by or when we are standing on or near its borders. Places and times of liminality (such as twilight or dawn) or turning places on the calendar (such as midwinter or midsummer) often provide access to Elfland, as do landscapes of wide vistas or colorful contrasts, such as Devon's Hound Tor, Arizona's Canyon de Chelly, or Brittany's Brociliande. In such places when time feels suspended, we are standing at the threshold of the Otherworld. Ritual (any act of sacred intention, such as painting, dancing, or the making of a poem) may provide entrance as well. Certainly, any place of feasting and revelry is sure to draw the attention of the faeries. Otherworldly denizens are often tied to particular cultures, landscapes, and sites, but learning to recognize the patterns of Otherworld imagery in one place at one site may help us recognize them in others. Repetition, pattern, and contrast in the landscape (three essential elements in faery stories) can be our best clues in detecting the borders of Elfland.

Because Faery is always present in some form, boundaries are often crossed by accident. This is why the old tales are so important: if you remember the stories, if you are familiar with the symbolic maps of the Otherworld, you already know something of the signs and rules of Faery. The right story is always the way out of the dark wood. We must carry stories with us in our pockets, like breadcrumbs, like compasses.

In addition to words of enchantment, in these pages you will find visions of the gates and their faery guardians. The guardians in the paintings, like the stories, are embodiments and expressions of the runes' traditional associations. A rune, a shard, an image, a sound, a memory—all these will help you enter the land of the telling. Cast about in your mind for clues. You may have encountered one of these landscapes before in a dream. The images and words you find in this book are not meant to stand alone. They are a beginning, a threshold. Once you cross the threshold, your own memories, creativity, and cleverness will open doors to other faery lands and experiences.

"Telling" the Runes

Reading and speaking are different kinds of acts. While we may convey information both ways, speaking out loud particularly affects the world around us and makes it resonate with our thoughts, feelings, and intentions. The Charms introducing each of the runes that follow should be spoken, chanted, sung, or whispered. Think about it this way: you are standing at the door of a friend's house, and there is no door knocker or bell. You have two choices: you might stand there until the door opens on its own (you may be waiting some time, so bring a snack), or you may call your friend's name out loud and ask to be let inside. Quiet is often associated with wisdom and contemplative learning, but creative use of song and voice may introduce you to other, equally wondrous experiences. Don't be afraid of your voice.

You may wish to speak the Tellings aloud as well. Speaking them may open other doors, or lead down other avenues for exploration. Feel how the vibrations of the words affect your body and your physical environment. How do they taste on your tongue? Let them live at the level of spoken language.

Like Elfland itself, the rune imagery and the Tellings may be quite different from your expectations. The Runes of Elfland tell their own stories on their own terms, stories both connected to and yet wildly different from mortal rune lore. Each chapter concludes with a Gift—words of wisdom, hints, and clues—to help you fully experience the inner meanings of the art and the stories.

Encounters with the Faery world always involve exchange. Balance keeps the borderland open for exploration; the exchange of gifts will help establish your developing relationship with the Otherworld. The images and stories may provide you with such gifts in the form of ideas, inspiration, knowledge and riddles to ponder. Think about your travels through the art and stories. Reflection upon such journeys is in itself another kind of journeying. Write down your adventures. Tell stories of your own experiences in the Faery landscapes. Paint pictures, use these images and stories as wellsprings for your own creative expressions of the Otherworld. Ally yourself with those who work to preserve natural places in the landscape. In these ways you join an ancient lineage of seers and custodians who give gifts back to the living land that continues to sustain us.

Marginalia, Artifacts, and Inscriptions

All the paintings in this book are filled with symbols, many of them related to artifacts of the ancient and medieval worlds. In the margins (though never marginal) are runic inscriptions, riddles, words of power, alphabetic bewilderments, and clues which may help you on your journey. Rune-treasures adorn some of the book's pages, part of the great hoard of Elfland. The creatures who romp and hide in the bindings and pages of this book may even form runes with their bodies. Even the smallest elf may point a finger in a sacred manner. We invite you to read between the lines.

In these artifacts and in the Gifts concluding each Rune are keys to their mythic and traditional associations. Such artifacts may tell their own stories. While it is not necessary to know their individual histories (though the Gifts will help point you in the right direction at times), their forms should be carefully studied. More important, these symbols may inspire you to create such artifacts yourself, or a telling of their origins as you perceive them to be. Turn them over in your mind and see what may be made of them. Keep an open and associative mind about you at all times: a sword may not always be a weapon. A cape could be the sky.

Seek, and sing of the treasures you shall surely find beyond the threshold: Carvings of the ancient gods of Elfland, totems of animal powers, carved stones, ancient fetishes, singing swords, shields and spirals, curious mechanisms, faery sewing kits, staves of wonder, shears of destiny, vessels of poetry and portent, alphabetic elves, crowns of inspiration, bones of heroes, spilling cauldrons, dark crystals, winding shrouds, raven armor, a cask of fortunes—and a hundred treasures more, hidden among the paintings.

How to Begin

All storytelling is a form of travel. All the things you know you should do when traveling in this world apply to Elfland as well. The Charms will open doors to strange and wondrous lands, so some travel tips and runic etiquette may be in order: Be polite. Don't take anything without asking. Laugh at their jokes. Remember, humor is sacred: so is hospitality. Beware of dark woods at night. Do not trust the wolf in winter. Take notes. Sing for your supper. Pack extra sandwiches. Bring fine gifts. Always tell a story when asked. Listen as if your life depended on it. Start early. Walk the land. Keep your eyes open. Travel wisely and well. Come back safe and sound.

How to begin?

Not hard to answer.

Choose a rune,

chant the charm,

tell the tale,

and step across.

A RUNE OF BEGINNINGS

THE CHARM

My song, the song
of catkin
shoot
and leaf
before their bloom,
and the sun
rising now through
limb and branch
to warm the wood
and draw the hidden sap
below the bark.

THE TELLING

Once and on the other side of the hedge, when the green mist rose, a girl walked through her garden gate and right out into the forest. She was of a walking mind and had a strong stride. She felt joy in the use of her legs, and sometimes she skipped, and sometimes she ran, and before she knew it, she was deep within the woods and lost. When she realized that she did not know the way home, she thought, and then she thought again, and said to herself, "I am here, for here I be, and what comes next I'll have to see."

Then on she walked, though the woods grew thick. Farther she skipped and the woods grew dark. She whistled to the birds, but the wrens only watched her in silence. She called out to the wolves, but they would not have her. She sang to the river, but the river ran from her. So on she went again past oak and ash, through night and morn, by low ground and high hill, and over the hump of noon until she came to a forest of birch trees. There an old woman with skin as white as the bark sat upon a stump by a spring.

The old woman spoke first, as was her right. "Welcome, daughter," said she with a voice dry as leaves. "A cool drink for a dry throat would be welcome indeed." Leaning down over the spring, the girl brought up water in a silver dish attached to a stone by a silver chain. The old woman was kind, and as she rose the trees inclined themselves towards her so that her ancient head was always in the shade. The old woman said, "Those who wander far are often thirsty." Gratefully the girl drank water from the spring in the forest of birch, and where she was once weary and sore, a great lightness and contentment filled her limbs.

The old woman, having no daughter of her own, asked her if she would like to stay within the forest for a time. This pleased the girl very much, and that is how she came to live in the forest of birch which stands at the very edge of Elfland, simple as that. The river whispered to her at night, and the roots came to know her name, and she was glad in their company. The Birch Mother became her mother, and the trees welcomed her with their watching eyes, and held her with their long, thin hands.

Now the Birch Folk are an ancient, private people, but they took her in and kept her as one of their own, and in time, she came to be more like them—long of arm, lithe, thin, and tall, with skin as white as their smooth bark and catkins woven through her hair. One day in early spring, the old woman left the woods without a word. The girl—who had much grown—became the Mother of the Birch Forest in her turn and watched over travelers who were in need and led children to the edge of the woods when they were lost. But for those who came to cut the trees, she had another face to show, though I will not speak of it here, for it was terrible indeed.

A full life she had within the woods, but how many years she remained among the trees cannot be reckoned, for trees count their years far more slowly than do we and in a manner all their own. Even on the edge of Elfland, time wends its own way; sometimes crawling, sometimes running. But after many years had passed, winter came upon her limbs, and slowly, slowly she wandered out of the woods and back along the path she had walked those many years ago.

Though she had been happy, ensconced within her tribe of trees, grown tall and strong, and finally old and wise with wood-lore, when she looked towards the garden gate a simple sorrow befell her. She found the gate much smaller now and all overgrown with briars.

But opening the gate again she feels the green mist rise and move with her across the garden. She begins to run toward the house, and seeing the windows open, she stands on her toes to peek inside the place where she was born. Looking in, she cannot remember how she had come to the forest, or how long she had been gone, or that she had been gone at all. She sees only her chair by the hearth, and knows that she is home.

And this tale is called Green Girl of the Birches, and there is a beginning and an end of it.

THE GIFT
The Birch Rune of Elfland encompasses the cycle of birth right through to burial, and all the joys and bumps in the road along the way. The guardian of this Rune is the Birch Woman and, depending on season or whim, she may appear as young or old. She is very friendly to children and provides protection for them especially. Her realm is very wide indeed, for any action performed for the first time may invoke her, and she attends with joy all moments of transition in the lives of folk who maintain their relationship with the natural world.

This Rune's signature is the birch tree itself, long used to make cradles and one of the first trees to leaf after winter. The birch is a sacred tree in every land where it grows. The oldest stories say it sprang from the tears of a girl. It is the Rune of Beginnings. The first forest of the world was a birch wood (called a birket by some), for the birch is a pioneer tree, rooting first into the land exposed by the receding ice sheets in the long and ago and before the warm green world was made. This Rune opens the gate to that first forest. Any ancient wood may also be a door, but these are hard to find in the world in these times, so even paper, common, but so like the bark of these trees, may be used to bolster any charm of setting out or growing up.

All the wondrous woods are within us, but we must journey out into the world to find them. The origins of the shapes of all things grow in this forest, and the guardian shapes her body to the rune as a reminder of this simple truth. This is not redundant but essential—we embody our origins and are shaped by all experiences that flow from the moment we begin our adventures in the wide world. She reminds us that Elfland can exist at the bottom of every garden and we have but to begin our journey with a bold, glad heart to find the gate open and the path to the woods waiting.

A RUNE OF SKILL

THE CHARM

From the perilous mound
I rise renewed as
Lord of Talents
First Revealer
Master of Revels
Splendor at noon
Golden
Youthful
seven sights
in my bright eye.

THE TELLING

The Sun was the first traveler, you know. Where he stops, he leaves his mark upon the stones, and all travelers still bear his blessing when they journey forth by day.

So it was a young man of noble bearing set out at noon for the house of the king, the sun upon his shoulder. Now the king bore a grievous wound. Great was the concern for him, for the fate of a king and the fate of the land are often one and the same. At this time, no one was admitted to the king without some special talent or skill that might bring him ease or extend the reputation of his court. So when the young man arrived, the porter asked his profession before he said, "Hello," before he called, "Welcome," before he asked, "What is your business?" Most irregular.

Standing on the threshold, his red hair lit from behind like a corona about his head, the young lord said he was a wood-wright and could work the boards with grace and skill.

"We have one most fine already," replied the porter, somewhat rudely.

"I am also a smith under whose hands rough metals glow and become ploughs, axes, spears, and swords. There is none better," said the lord, smiling a smile that showed all his bright teeth to advantage.

"We are pleased with our smith and do not need another, even with such a smile as yours."

"I am a bull of battle, a champion on the field. Many are my victories."

" Hmmm," said the porter, "bull indeed, and very impressive, but not needed. All within this hall are heroes thrice exalted, even the women."

"You have not yet heard my lines," said the young lord, who began to clear his throat.

But the porter said, "We have poets and wag-tongues enough to fill the place."

"Harper?"

"Already got one."

"Teacher of lore?"

"O young redundant, thou."

"Magician?"

"Ten might be conjured away and we would still have plenty."

"Very well, with so fine a hall as this, you must need a warrior. I can watch the road and defend it, and my arm is very long with sling and spear."

"The road is clear—except for yourself—and is well watched already. We do not need you."

"Leech?"

"Not another doctor."

"Bronze master?"

"Good day, young sir."

"Cup bearer?"

"No, but I will raise a glad glass at the sight of your back," said the bold porter.

"Wait!" replied the youth, smiling broadly once again, "Have you one man who is all these things at once?"

Well now, at this the porter paused and put his glass back down again. He shifted his weight from heel to heel, and, without another word he turned and hurried to the king's hall, carrying his news from the gate. So, this young man with the bright teeth was finally invited in and was set a task before the company. Could he fling a flagstone the size of ten bulls over a wall? A curious request, but small work indeed for such a youth as he. Might he play the harp to please a weary king? This was his special excellence, and play he did until the king's court wept as at a funeral, until they cheered like an army victorious, and until their hearts were clean swept away upon notes that flew like birds into the air from the youth's clever fingers.

The stars were rising when the splendid music finally faded. The king, whose own heart had been warming toward the youth since his arrival, invited him to sit at his side in the chair of sages, and offered his throne to him for thirteen days. The young lord accepted. In that small time he defeated the king's ancient enemies and got for himself a glorious name in the bargain. He lived a life full of adventure, for he fought and loved and wandered the world, making a bonfire of his every action, lighting the minds of poets and bards, who still sing his name with awe. And when he died, some say before his time, his body was placed within the Hill of the Sun, for son of the sun he was.

THE GIFT

A warrior, wanderer and master of skills, the Sun is a frequent guest in Elfland, for he revels there at the end of each day, drinking deep and sleeping fast and sure below the ground. Weary at the end of his long year, upon the eve of midwinter, the night of hope and flame, he enters the hollow mounds of Elfland and is there restored by powerful rites unknown to mortal eyes and unrecorded in mortal lore.

The carved stone at the entrance to the burial mound at Newgrange in Ireland bears spirals upon it. From an engraved center line, they turn away to the left and to the right. The middle of these opposite-turning spirals aligns with the entrance to the ancient tomb, the place where the Sun God enters and exits the earth. In Ireland, faery mounds such as Newgrange are called "sun bowers," and these monuments are constructed to admit the sun's light upon the solstices, the great festivals that hinge the year. A door to Elfland is open whenever light enters the earth or the lightning of illumination strikes a darkened mind.

To move clockwise, also called the "sun-wise turn," is always lucky and it will bring good fortune to you in times of need. To sanctify the moment, make this turn around a building, an object, a person, or a monument, by heading south towards the sun and keeping the object to your right as you travel the circuit around it. This is an ancient blessing custom, but in reverse it has long been known to open a perilous road into the darker halls of Elfland. Circuits made widdershins, counter-clockwise, bring bad luck at all times.

As the source of order, this guardian should be invoked when a new task or journey is begun or when a new talent is obtained or when oaths and solemn promises are made. To call this guardian to watch over you upon your road, walk a circuit in his own manner and, making this Rune upon the ground at the quarters of your path, look up to find him walking with you.

23

A RUNE OF PROTECTION

THE CHARM

May I stand
as an island in the marsh
as a hill in the plain
as a tree on the elfmound
as a star in the moon's waning
as a still sword in the hand
as a child beloved of its ancestors
in the midst of the grove
brave before the host.

THE TELLING

There is a shard of a story, still told among the marsh-folk, of a young girl come to claim her father's sword. He had lain long in his barrow and his bones were clean and gleaming in the earthlight, and his sword was there with him, cold and waiting. He was longed for by his people, loved and revered by his daughter, but all the land was on fire in his absence. This is why she had come; enemies from beyond the sea, a land defenseless. This much could be guessed at, for it is the beginning of a hundred tales. But here is something strange. The sword she sought was not forged by men. Even in her father's father's father's time, that sword was already an old thing, for it had come from within the hollow hills, forged by fair hands in the dark backward and abysm of time.

So she came to the marsh, where strange lights move above the waters and polished trunks of trees attend the ground like bones. Following the lights she came to the barrow mound and found the dead were waiting for her. The sword was hers, they said, but she would need

to know how to wield it. She would save the land, they said, if the sword was held aright. There were voices among the long sharp reeds and they told to her a very great secret, a thing fit for only her to know. But I'll tell you now, and who knows? Perhaps some good may come of it. *This sword must never be raised in anger and must never strike a foe. On that day the sword will break and sink again into the earth. The weapon must be held aloft, borne in silence by ancestral blessing.*

And so it was done.

She returned to her land and did as she was bid. And the armies saw the sword of Elfland raised and heard the sword begin to sing. And her enemies withdrew in silence and the fires on the land were quenched, for who can stand against the will of Elfland when it is roused by the hands of a clever girl? Thus the sword found its keeper. She would, as it pleased her, lend this great gift to men who swore to keep the land in peace, but always the sword fell away from them and found its way back into the earth and back to her hand. So at last she left it to her daughter, and she to hers. So even now if you wish to learn the secret of the sword (for she is loath to lend it of late), you must seek the Woman of the Marsh—though you may know her by another name—and promise not to use it.

THE GIFT

This Rune and the sword itself embody defense in all their aspects. History tells of far too many times when swords were wielded as weapons, the war songs sung, and blood flowed freely on the land. But within this Rune lies a rare and secret irony: defense may come not from raising the sword but by leaving it still. A battle cannot be without two sides willing to fight. As an emblem of ancestral support and faery solidarity, this Rune rises from the waters every time a war may be won by not waging war.

There are many faery swords. But remember, traditionally it is the scabbard rather than the sword that holds the most magic. Often, the real danger only comes to the wielder when the sword is drawn in aggression, or when the scabbard is lost or forgotten—in those times when we forget to put our anger away.

True protection exists within silences, when a harsh word is not spoken. Speak the word "Peace" to this guardian in any tongue and she lays the sword of Elfland at your feet, a sign that valor may be concealed in stillness; there we find a sacred enclosure, a place of safety in-between actions, an island in the sea. Avalon.

A RUNE OF JOURNEYS

THE CHARM

Away, come away!
The great wheel is turning
the wind is awakened
this day is for walking
on secret lanes known
to our glad eyes alone.
Night falls,
moon calls
our old hearts leap
with love of the road.
Come away!

THE TELLING
We have always been traveling folk. We journey in the mouth of the night, and on the cross-quarter days of the year we move house, traveling between one *rath* (or faery fort) and another. We are quiet about our business, keeping to our own roads. We love the old tracks best and they must never be blocked, so it's best to leave your doors open on the traveling days, just in case. If you're lucky, you will not know that we have passed, for sometimes your folk are carried off by the Gentry and what becomes of them few can say. Stranger still, every now and again one of the Good People, one of our own, gets lost, left behind in a strange and foreign country. This happened long ago, at the place once called Wolf Pits. Even mortals will tell you it is true, for it is.

Yes, we are all travelers, but I am the one who was left.

Bells were ringing—that is what I remember—and the music was irresistible. My brother and I were traveling with our father's flocks, but we left to follow the bells instead.

We walked up the valley on an old, forgotten path, towards an opening in the torn hillside. Feeling the sides of the cave with our hands, we wandered into the tolling, into the music of the bells. We walked on in the darkness and the ringing became a feeling, a desire, until it stopped suddenly. Then a brilliant light was all about us, at our faces, burning our eyes, and we fell.

When we awoke, wet fallen leaves were on our skins. The land was strange to us, the sky was brighter, and we could no longer hear the bells. The cave from which we'd come now resembled only a shallow hole in the hill. The unwashed found us then, and we were entreated to follow these large, dirty folk towards a village. We followed, though we could not discern the meaning of their words, which were harsh and foreign to our ears.

We were hungry, and after a time, some beans were brought to us. An ancient woman with thick, soft hands pulled the pods in half and spilled the peas out. We ate them without thinking, and so were trapped in that far country. We were hungry and foolish, and had forgotten that to eat the food of a foreign land binds you to that place. Such bonds are not easily broken, but my brother was braver than I.

Some time later, the hue of our skin became like theirs and my brother fell ill. He did not stay long in that strange land and when at last he grew silent, I knew he had returned to our people's twilight country on a dark road I did not wish to take.

I am the one who stayed behind. My brother has gone back to the hill. When on a Traveling Day the wind rises up, carrying fallen leaves out across the gray world, and bells are ringing in the earth, I will follow him home.

THE GIFT

An old faery lullaby from the Highlands begins, "I would range the night, through wood, through heath." And if you wish to find the gates to Elfland, you will have walk as well. The shape of this Rune implies the motion of walking, and indeed, travel on foot is the surest way to find the Faery realm. When walking, we move more slowly, see the ground, hear our feet upon it and the sound of the hollow earth beneath them. Our attentions are held by the living world around us: we pass between the trees and suddenly find ourselves within their land.

When drawing this Rune we are taken up like leaves on the wind, carried along with the Faery host. Beware. Also inherent in this Rune is the ancient elvish prank of being "pixie-led." When you are in well-known territory but suddenly lose your way, wandering off into the land, you'll know the pixies are having a laugh at your expense. You can turn your pockets inside out to end the ordeal, but there may be a lesson to be learned in this. It's easy to take the land for granted, especially places familiar to us. When we are pixie-led, we begin to walk differently. Everything looks new and strange. We spiral through the countryside, crossing our own path many times. When we are lost, our senses become fully engaged and we begin to truly see again.

This Rune encourages us to find the subtle roads on the land. These paths are aligned to larger patterns such as the road of the sun, the trackways of the dead, and the invisible lines existing between ancient places on the land: ruins, old churches, standing stones and circles, and faery hills most especially. These roads are only navigable by adjusting our perception. We must learn to be aware of the significance of such places, to be able to detect and travel the shining roads between them. This Rune also acknowledges any creature who helps us find our road, or who accompanies or aids us upon our travels; the dogs of this world or the Other, as hunters, guides, and friends.

To find the road of this Rune and meet its guardians, find a forked rod of hazel and cut this Rune upon it. Begin walking. Journey with intention, as a pilgrim, but do not think too hard upon your destination or your return.

A RUNE OF FORTUNE

THE CHARM

Where are you?
Candle of evening
mistress of games,
the stone is lifted.
Horns of heaven
helper of travelers,
your path is sure.
Cask of fortune
caller of tides,
walk with us.
Keeper of the cup and ring,
you are free.

THE TELLING
In Elfland, the Moon has a hundred names, but the most sacred and secret name (which must not be written in mortal characters) is translated to mean "marker of years," evidence of both her high status and the existence of elvish lunar timekeeping. Indeed, the Moon is a very great goddess among them. She is also a wanderer, and even in the distant borderlands of Faery, strange tales are told of the walking Moon. Many times have I stumbled through the fens looking for her, trying to improve my fortunes. For the Moon is the mother of luck, you know, though once, long ago and every now and then, bad luck attends her too. Just there, among the reeds and rushes, in the quaking bogs, the Moon has gotten lost.

I was there one night when the Moon covered her head and walked among the marshes. I saw her misstep and the great stone that tipped up and fell upon her, holding her beneath the water. I heard the *wykes* come and the fen-worms, saw the way they held her

down and saw the night go dark and the evil creatures rise up, brave in the absence of the Moon. I waited for her at the edge of the bog, but she did not come. I put straw in my hat, cast lots, consulted the bones, and read the signs, but to no avail. The comings and goings of the Moon are not a man's business, I suppose. So I asked the old woman what to do. She gave me a pebble to put in my mouth, and a pearl to place in my pocket, handed me a hazel wand to hold as I walked, and sent me back to the bog-lands in silence to find the stone and lift it. I did all that and found the Moon. I saw the light dance from beneath the dark water and broke the stone that held her fast, but she is still a wanderer and my luck is as it always was.

THE GIFT
The traditional meanings of this Rune are obscure—lost long ago from the mortal lore, like the Moon herself on that strange night—but if we seek its meaning in Elfland, it may be found. There, all things tied to chance are children of the Moon. She is the protectress of any who travel between dusk and dawn, the mistress of creatures who dance within the dark of evening, and patroness of anything that brightens or dims, or ebbs and flows, love and fortune most especially. She is therefore always present at the lover's window and the gaming table, anywhere risks are taken and lots are cast.

Even now the Moon goes walking and is lost to us for a time. Or more likely in these strange days, you may simply forget to look up, forget to gaze at the Moon—though her light is lovely on your face—and so find yourself in darkness. Go to the wise woman; you'll know her when you see her. Ask for a stone, a branch of hazel, a pearl of wisdom. Go quietly without a word and find the moon you've lost. When you see her again, make a song of her names. Sing it in her spilling light. Or curtsey to the Moon on a Monday, or use a reed to make this Rune in milk upon the ground three hours after twilight. If her aspect is favorable, she will open her cask and the fortune you seek or deserve will attend you.

A RUNE OF WEALTH

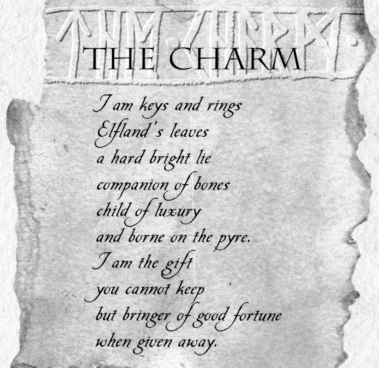

THE CHARM

I am keys and rings
Elfland's leaves
a hard bright lie
companion of bones
child of luxury
and borne on the pyre.
I am the gift
you cannot keep
but bringer of good fortune
when given away.

THE TELLING
Long and ago and before today, there were riches hidden beneath every hill. Some of this has been talked about by fools, and little good has come of it, for anything stolen out of Elfland bears a price too dear for most to pay.

It is true that a burial mound still stands not far from here, and once it was filled with faery gold. At one time music could be heard rising from that place at night, and it was known that the hill was hollow. Chests of treasure had been buried there many ages ago, and for almost as long, people had tried to get them out again. One night not long ago, two lads went up the hill to claim the gold and burrowed down into the mound like badgers. They dug deep, and deeper still, moving rock and soil one shovel at a time. This took most of the night, for the earth is slow to give up its riches, but sometime before sunrise a large chest was discovered, heavy with gold, sturdy with bronze bands about it and large bronze rings at each side. Clever as they were in their greed, the youths decided that a rope should be placed

through these rings and one of them would pull the chest up from above, while the other pushed from below. So that is what they did, but as the chest reached the top of the hole, one of the rings broke free. The chest fell back down into the ground, crushing one fellow beneath it, and the sides of the pit caved in, burying everything under the dark soil.

The luckier of the two ran fast and soon returned with help. For three days no sound was heard at the hill but the scraping of shovels against hard stone and soft earth. Nothing was found, neither lost lad nor lost gold, and so all the earth was shoveled back and a loaf of bread was left atop the hill for good measure.

Two went to the hollow hill but only one returned. And he came away with only a single ring of bronze to remind him of that night. What's become of the ring I do not know. This much I can tell you: no one has dug there since. Indeed, few will even visit that place, for now a low and doleful sigh is often heard coming from within the tump at night. All other music is gone from that hill.

THE GIFT

In Elfland, wealth is reckoned differently than it is among mortals. Gold has little value in and of itself. No doubt such baubles are kept by the elves because they delight the eye and do not tarnish or diminish with the passing of time.

On very rare occasions, faeries may make a gift of gold or other money to a mortal. This may be kept, but it must never be spoken of, for upon the day the gift is mentioned, it will turn to earth or rubbish in your hand. Generally, though, faery money ought not be trusted, as it often turns to leaves in the sunlight. Therein is a lesson about the true nature of wealth.

This Rune reminds us that some treasures are more valuable when they are left in the ground. For many thousands of years, both elves and our ancestors worked to fill the earth with wonders: golden torques, singing swords, resplendent chalices, bright carved gems gleaming with light of sun and moon. But these are not for you. They are gifts to the dead, sacrifices to the hill-gods of old, placed in the ground for the sake of remembrance. The real gifts of Elfland are not found within the earth but in the heart, in song, dance, revelry, cleverness, fond memories of the past, and the love of the land for its own sake aside from the hidden riches of its depths.

Draw this Rune in mud or leaf mold on your own eager hand every time you forget the difference between what you own and what owns you.

A RUNE OF COMPANIONSHIP

THE CHARM

When you dream of the well
or the world turned upside down
or the dust behind the door
or hear your name
when no one can be seen,
seek the mirror
below the earth
where realm meets realm
and you will find me waiting.

THE TELLING

You are falling asleep again. Or perhaps you're just waking up. It is difficult to tell sometimes. We are surrounded by mists when we wake and forget so much of our travels, but this much I can tell you: we are not alone in this world, or the Other. In dreams too, those in-between lands, our Other-self waits for us. The co-walker, or Fetch, is a most ancient and curious kind of faery. We each have one assigned to us when we enter this world and it fades away when we depart our lives. It occasionally walks at our sides, but is generally invisible to our waking eyes.

This may be for the best, for some believe that to see the Fetch anyplace other than in a dream, to meet your Other-self in the waking world, is ominous and may portend dangers of the worst kind. Of course, death is but another way to see the world. And none of this may worry you too greatly if you have heard of the man who, seeing his own Fetch approaching, shouted, "What are you doing here?" and berated the poor thing so badly that it skulked

away in shame. Still, it may be safer to seek it in the Otherworld, where the Fetch's appearance is not limited only to moments that stand between a person and his last breath. The Fetch makes its home in Elfland, where the wise speak of it as the first guide a visitor is likely to meet there. Because Fetches have become so shy in these times, it is best for you to seek yours out and introduce yourself properly, face to face.

Here is how it may be done:

It is said that there are precisely four-hundred and eighty-seven distinct and reliable entrances into Elfland, but only one of them leads to the Fetch, and this is true. Now you could try them all, one after the other, or you might simply wait until a leap year or a cross-quarter day, when all doors to Faery except for two are closed for maintenance. It is during these rare times that the Fetch's favorite haunt is most easily attained. So you will have to choose one of the two doors. Pick carefully. One way will lead you the Park of Posterity, where white-bearded, three-headed faery pensioners sit upon benches and regale the already-weary listener with tales of their youthful exploits as grease captains in the Goblin Guard. The other door, and this is the one you want, I promise you, leads straight to the sewers.

This is the habitation of the Fetch, far below the surface, where the waters of the world wind down into the earth. Since all the water tracks in Elfland eventually find their way to this place, it is logical to assume that any journey, any adventure, may begin here as well. Do not be shocked by the Fetch's appearance, for he is the only denizen of Elfland who will show you his true face on the first meeting; like you, he has little shame.

When you arrive, the Fetch will catch you with one open eye and look at you intently with his lure-helmet aquiver. Meet his gaze and stare back, standing on one foot. He will open his other eye and stare even more intently. Raise one arm and keep staring back. This game will soon become tiresome. If you tell him so, he will finally get around to asking you his riddle, though he may tell you to keep standing on one foot with your arm raised because you look funny like that.

Here is the riddle of the Fetch:

Not your face, nor your hair.

Not a piece of the pieces of your trunk.

I am upon you, though you are no heavier.

What am I?

The answer to this is your price of admission into Faery.

If you answer correctly, Elfland's door of reflection will be open to you and the Fetch, your most willing companion and guide to the lower worlds.

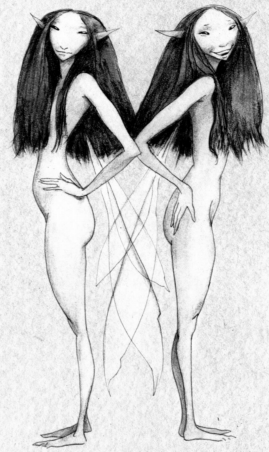

THE GIFT
In the lands of the Far North, the Fetch are called the *fylgjur* and usually only appear in dreams or in waking times of imminent danger. So the Fetch may be a kind of personal guardian, or faery friend, watching over its charge throughout the course of his or her lifetime.

The shape of this Rune signifies a person gazing at himself, and hints that the deeper nature of this guardian is found in duality and recognition. The absurd appearance of the Fetch is essential to its character, and to yours. Wherever laughter is lacking, so is humanity.

The Fetch is us, our reflection in the Otherworld, our faery shadow. And to find your faery guardian is to rescue your hidden nature from obscurity. That true self is a wellspring, often hidden deep below the surface but well worth the finding, for its pure flow is sustenance to you and those around you, even in times of drought.

This guardian invites us to drink from the Springs of Comitatus which percolate below the palaces of Elfland, to see our reflection in those waters, and to recognize the deep ancestral streams always at work within us. This door to Elfland lives inside of us, through the remembrance of family, friends, and community, in the privilege of trusted companions, in the knowledge that we are never alone on our life's journey.

A RUNE OF MEMORY

THE CHARM

I place my foot
upon the hollows of home
and remember
the girl who took back her name,
a fool who found the cup,
women who watch the wells,
strong sisters striding from the ruins.
All the folk of earth-fast stone,
their rising names
in winter tales retold,
are giants in the making.

THE TELLING

The stones have always been here, though the stories of the names carved upon them are often lost to us. The yew remembers them, though, and keeps them close, winding its roots tight about the bones of the dead. If you tend the earth around its trunk, a story may rise up, wet with mold, an old tale, long buried within the vaults of loam. This is exalted ground indeed, for giants are buried here, and their tale is still worthy of the telling.

Two giants come, bound, to the house of a king. Their eyes reflect the old land and its past. Their blood is bold with battles and songs. Dark-eyed, broad-armed, heartstrong: the giant sisters are held as prisoners in the house of the king. Just how this king caught them is known by no tongue, though some say he tricked them to learn of their names. He wants only their strength, knowing naught of their nature. He puts them to work: he tricks them and keeps them, binding their strong hands to the shaft of his mill. They walk there in

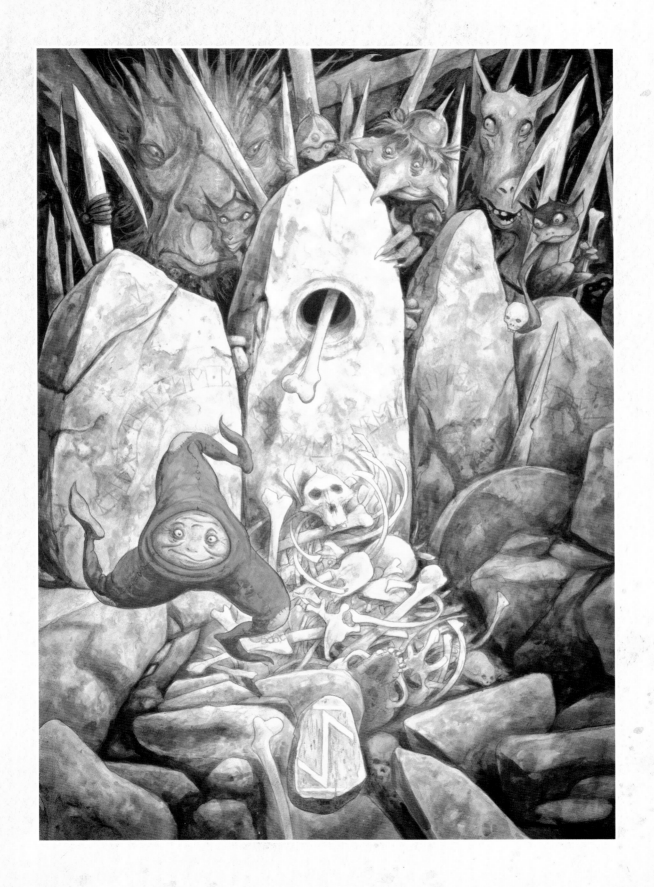

45

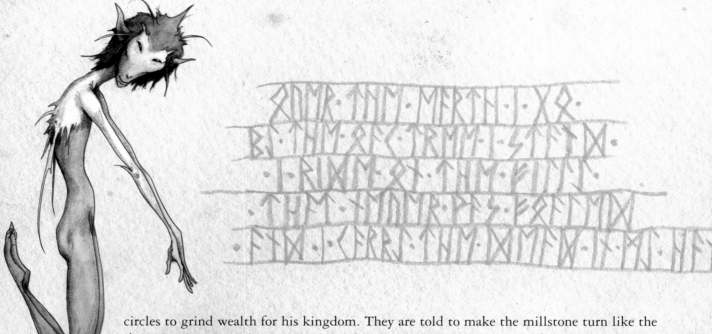

circles to grind wealth for his kingdom. They are told to make the millstone turn like the sky. No pleasure is theirs, no rest, no distraction. The mill must not be still, the stone never idle with their hands at the shaft.

To mill without pause is folly and foolish; to work without rest brings bad fortune indeed. Now these bold girls know of the fissures held deep in the millstone, know, too, how best to preserve it from harm. "Let us stop the great stone!" they cry out to the king. "Just a few moments still, to save it from cracking." But the king commands motion. The king commands them to grind without cease.

There is no silence in the mill house, the great stone singing as it swings to its work. This song continues until sleep comes upon them. All but the giants sleep sound in that hall. But no anger boils in the bellies of the giants; no enmity works in those prisoners' hard hearts. They say to each other, "We shall grind wealth for this king. Wealth will whirl from the glorious mill. On treasure he'll sit, a bed of gold will be his. He shall wake only to joy by the work of our hands. But the gold shall come to be held by others, and his name shall be grist for the mill. Only then shall all be well ground." And wealth pours forth from the work of their stone.

No answer to his fortune does the king make upon waking; no comment makes he on his mill's goodly gold. "Do not stop working!" is his only cry. "Your rest is no longer than these, my words." Then he leaves them to work. No thanks are given, no kindness made, not a thought for the mill's ancient dames.

The giants don't cease, they keep the mill wheel in motion, but cry out with words of warning and woe:

"All kings have power, but this one's a fool. A wise one would think more of the fate of his name. A poor deal you brokered, bringing us to this hall. You chose us for strength, well done, but asking our ancestry would have been wiser.

"There are kings, there are kinsmen of power that move in our blood. We once raised gold cups with warriors and gods. Old giants of earth there are in our family, and long they've been honored. You would have done better to ask first of them.

"The mountain of stone gave you this mill, this wheel of stone we spin like a spell. No stone serves you unless it is willing. No giant's daughters shall work against their will.

"My sisters and I grew up in the earth. We moved bedrock at breakfast, and supped below ground. Our travels were wide over the giant's domain. The earth shook with the weight of our wandering. People were larger in times long ago. Dead kings became gods, not at all like today.

"Many names we were called by, many honors were ours: Shield-Breakers, Warrior's-Winter, Overturner-of-Thrones, to name but a few. Our blades ran red in those days; we threw spears made of logs, bore hammers like boulders across the wide world.

"Yet in this king's house, we are shown no respect. We are held as prisoners, our names forgotten, our gifts insulted. But soon we shall rest. Soon will the stones fall silent and still. Now we shall sing a hard fate for this king. From our words flow invasion. Our flour, the blood that flows forth from a war. Even now your neighbors rise up against you! Even now your brothers call out for your death. Your frontiers are on fire, and flames run to greet you. Your name will be nothing, by no one honored. This is the fortune that comes from your deeds! Wake up, mighty king! Wake up, little man! Wake up to hear the dark song of your fate."

Now battles are blazing, a harrowing host marching fast to that hall. Now a hard fate is ground for the king at his mill. Now the millstone is flying, a terrible tempest, turned by the giants with strong blood in their veins. They keep the stone turning, faster and faster; their words become wolves that stalk that high hall. The giants mill harder, until the shaft begins crying, bending and cracking at their furious pace. The shaft shakes. The stand breaks. The mighty mill bursts to pieces; fragments fly fast at the king's crumbling walls.

The mill is in ruins, stark silence attends it. The king's hall is shattered and covered with ash. The giants call out as they stride from the pile: "Now, king, we are finished with work for your kingdom; too long have we toiled with work at your mill. This hall is now fallen. Your name lies beneath it. A bone yard, a blank stone, such is your fate."

THE GIFT It is true, the yew tree is the guardian of the graveyard. It is the keeper of the bones and epitaphs, and knows many secrets kept in Elfland but long lost to living memory. Like the yew, this guardian teaches that death belongs to life. Indeed, they may be one and the same, for if we live in a manner worthy of remembrance, we live forever in the hearts of those who speak our names with love and honor.

The houses of bone and places of burial lie very close to Elfland and are deeply storied landscapes. Some of their tales are lost. Others inspire such frequent tellings that the names they hold become exalted in successive generations. This is how giants are born, you know, in the glorious tales of those who have gone before. The story of the giant sisters has been told for a thousand years, but the names of such petty kings as this one are forgotten, left rotting in the leaf mold of the forest of tales—a warning to others who value wealth above hospitality, or cannot spare a moment to honor the past.

To find Elfland's gate of honor, form the Rune with yew branches by a place of bones, recite the charm, and sing of the adventures of a beloved ancestor. Make them noble in the telling, paint their praises brightly, use words of gold to make them great. Then go from that place and live a life worthy of its own tale.

A RUNE OF PROPHECY

THE CHARM

Here is vision and voice,
a pale hand raised in warning,
an empty seat in the high hall,
absence of the old wise ways,
blind eyes seen through the silent shroud.
Shall I speak more?
Grow silent?
Sink down?
Nothing frees us from fate.

THE TELLING
I hear him riding to the eastern door. The king of Elfland dreams of his own death. I see this. He hears the night birds calling his name about the copse. I have heard them. He feels the earth grow cold as he rides to me, feels the question hold his heart like stone: when will my time come?

When he arrives, we will begin an ancient game.

He will call me from the ground—pull an old woman out of bed! Where has courtesy fled in these dark days? He will use the old ways, speak the charms, call the names, ask me to see for him what should be left alone, and sing of things that should remain in silence. The future rides towards us fast enough, I'll tell him, though he will not believe it. A king should be easier with his wyrd.

Then he will bow low, call me "gracious crone," and "wise one," and "good mother." He will ask again about his dream, about the faery maidens who wail and cry and pull

49

their hair by the vacant royal chair. He will not wait for me to answer but will beg to learn the meaning of the cold bench draped in purple and pall, hidden in the dark hall below the hills of Elfland. "Who will sit there?" he will ask, as if he wants to hear the answer. So he will wheedle me with fair words. Always the same. Poetry before threats. He will offer praise, promise gossip, treasure, stories from the outer world, tellings of the green lands, sweet songs to soften my cracking lips, a new veil woven on elvish looms. What use have I for such things?

He may try spell-craft to pull the visions from me. You see? Even the great are fools in the face of fate. When I tell him of the futility of his quest, and I will, he will call me names. Hag. Witch. Mother of Monsters. He will not be the first. So I will tell him what he already knows: *The hungry ground waits for us all.* And he will leave no wiser than he came.

"Enough, enough..." I'll tell him then. "Go back to your bowers of the sun. Live your days. Love your children. Do not seek more." He thinks because I'm blind I see the future clearly, when in fact I am blind because I'm old. And old as I am, I have learned to take things as they come.

THE GIFT
This Rune opens doors to the faery Closet of Constraint, and to the Halls of Hesitation, and to the Oubliette of Obscurity, where great and foolish questions are asked that deserve no answer. This guardian appears whenever we work against nature by striving to know too much. She tells us that true vision is granted by living *through* our difficult experiences, not in trying to avoid them through the use of prophecy and fortune telling. The improper use of the second sight or the words of prophets may make us slaves to our wyrd, or fate. Once we think we know the future, we may forget that we have yet to play a significant role in making it. Any time we abandon free will for obsession, this gate is open to us.

The Rune takes its shape from the bow drill, implying that we must respond to adversity with practical, simple action. When great pestilence is upon the land, old folklore tells of using a bow drill to make the need-fire, which is then used to cure cattle of their illness. This is a memorial action, using archaic technology, an act of respect that reminds people of their connections to hallowed and hard-won knowledge. Such memories of the past, of the tried and true, often hold clues to our current dilemmas, enabling us to play a part in the resolution of difficulties that have no foreseeable outcome.

This guardian, who is the Sybil of Elfland, holds the knowledge of everything we refuse to accept or would be better off not knowing. Approach her with great care. She already knows you are coming.

A RUNE OF EXCHANGE

THE CHARM

At the entrance to the hollow earth
we weave the worlds together
by promise
by bargain
by bond
by words spoken over stone.
We are the joy at
the handshake of all
good neighbors.

THE TELLING
A kettle must have three legs to stand, so three stories you shall have.

Once and upon an island there lived a farmer's wife who owned a kettle, and every day a woman of the faery folk would come to borrow it. No words would she speak, but when the faery lifted up the kettle, the woman of the house would say:

Cold iron is heated with coals
the cost of the kettle is bones
and to return it full and whole.

And every day the kettle was returned, full of good meat and bones for broth. Now this went on for some time—for both women were well pleased with the arrangement—until the woman of the house had to be away. She left her husband with instructions, but you already know that no good came of that. When he saw the faery woman coming, with a shadow from

her feet, he closed the door and would not open it. No open door did she need, for as soon as the faery woman approached the threshold of the house, the kettle began to jump, once, twice, and the third time it flew up and out at the roof ridge. Night fell and the kettle did not return. The woman of the house came back and gave harsh of her tongue for her husband's foolishness. He swore the faery would return, but the wife knew better. So she hastened to the knoll and seeing no one within, went in herself. The Gentry of the hill were all out hunting after their suppers and, seeing the kettle unguarded, she took it up, though it was heavy with the remains of their meal. Now one faery was left within the knoll and when he saw her going out with the kettle, he called:

Silent wife, silent wife
Who comes here from the land of the living,
beware the dogs of the hill!
Now Dark goes free, and Fierce follows after!

And so she ran, and two faery dogs ran after her. A fourth of the food she threw to them to make them pause, and they did. But they soon took up after her and another handful she threw at them. She walked as quickly as she could and when she got close to home, she overturned the pot on the earth. The faery dogs stopped then, and the dogs of the village took up barking, and soon she was safely home, but the faery woman from the knoll never sought the kettle again, and many a hungry night was known thereafter by both wife and husband.

Now that woman got her own back from the knoll, although she lost much in the adventure—such accords, once broken, are seldom mended. But that was not the only mound to have faery gifts within it, ready to trade or lend or give to those who could keep a compact. I have heard of another kettle, a cauldron in fact, that once belonged to the elves and is now resting in a church, a strange place for it indeed. The mound from which it came was a marvel, for it was known that if you entered that hollow place, you would find a long stone and, knocking upon it, you might ask to borrow whatever you would like. For a year or more you might keep the gift of it: money, a tool, a flute, a yoke for oxen, a spurtle, anything. Knock, declare what you would have, state when you would return it, and that was all that need be done. A voice would then announce when you might return to the mound to claim your gift, and on the appointed day it would be found upon the stone as promised. This was an ancient practice, but once a cauldron was borrowed from the mound and not returned according to the promise, and though it was brought back many times after, the mound-folk would not accept it. Never again was anything lent from that hill.

While that mound is still silent, many other places of gift-giving and borrowing yet exist upon the land, many places where discretion and politeness may still bring good fortune. Any farmer knows this, one in particular whose story is well worth the telling. He was a - good man, a clever man who kept his hearth clean, and always had a pail of sweet water at the ready for company, and left a dish of cream out at night for good measure.

The tale runs thus:

One day as he is coming home from the fields, he finds the faery market open for business, stalls bright as can be. Well, he walks up to one of the stalls and very kindly asks to see a cider mug that is hanging there. A price is agreed upon and out comes the farmer's money, and instead of coins for change, the elves give him dried leaves with all formality. So it's all

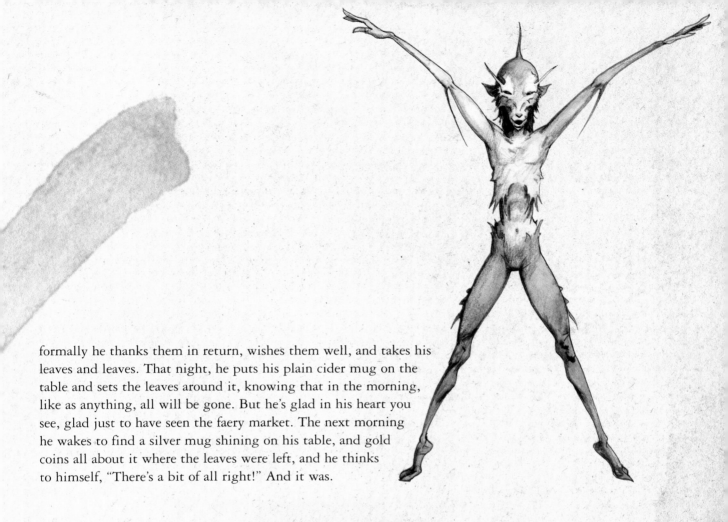

formally he thanks them in return, wishes them well, and takes his
leaves and leaves. That night, he puts his plain cider mug on the
table and sets the leaves around it, knowing that in the morning,
like as anything, all will be gone. But he's glad in his heart you
see, glad just to have seen the faery market. The next morning
he wakes to find a silver mug shining on his table, and gold
coins all about it where the leaves were left, and he thinks
to himself, "There's a bit of all right!" And it was.

THE GIFT
There are a hundred more tales of goodly gifts given out
of Elfland, but there is much dust upon such stories and the days of fair bartering with
the faeries seem to lie in the past. In their place are dark tales, tellings of times when
good sense was ignored, cups were stolen from the hills, and the old compacts were
forgotten or abused. In such times, Elfland will seek recompense in what ways it can,
and tradition is filled with faery blasts, withering of limbs, faltered bloodlines, and
buckets of milk turned bad.

But who is to say that we might not revive the tradition of trading with our Good
Neighbors? There are still many hollow hills, and many knocking stones, and many places
where music drifts among the stalls, and the entrance to the faery market may still be
found. If we recall the rules of barter, if we trade fairly and without deceit, and if we
remember that a little politeness is worth its weight in gold in Elfland, the ancient faery
gift gate may open again to us.

And if you find yourself at the rich stalls and barter halls of Elfland, come prepared to
trade. Sometimes they need the things we have: our milk, our butter, our kettles. But
more than this, Elfland needs us to be good neighbors, to spare a kind thought, to leave
a bit of cream by the door. Not because we hope to gain riches but because that is what
good neighbors do.

A RUNE OF MOTION

THE CHARM

Horse and Hattock!

THE TELLING Life is motion.

Always when you are riding, there are winds. Your hair, your clothes, the horse's mane and tail, all blow madly about in seemingly random gusts. And yet, even when blinded by the wind, the horse knows where she is going. If you trust her, you will come to your right destination.

So the winds of the world are about you. Each gust tells a portion of a different tale, carries you swiftly past brief and passing visions, fast and fading reflections of distant lives, whispers of varied songs sung long ago or far away or in the moment of your departure. If you are attentive, you may hear such stories or see such signs as are fit for you to know.

A westward wind bears to you a melody of ambivalence and beginnings. Here are notes from the birds of the Otherworld; the songs of love and war, of life and sleep. Here are the music of a mother's love, the sight of a familiar youth, and the lamentations at the gatepost when a child wanders forth into the world.

The south wind brings tidings of the summer land. Here flies an ancient actor's line spoken from behind a mask. Here the wind calls out like a chorus, *To you she spoke, and made her meaning plain. . .caught in the casting-net of destiny. . . .* Then it breaks away and is gone.

Easterly airs bear the sound of trumpets and the tidings of contention.   There are fragrances of excellent spices and rare flowers and bread, upon that wind, and the air of all desirous things. You hear calls of bartering and trade, the frantic barkings of the marketplace. Fading bells of caravans dissolve beneath the turning sky.

From the north, through the trees, are sightings of ravens and a chapel. A woman sits upon a stone, and beside the stone a flood of curious colors runs from the chapel out onto the land. Here are hounds and hawks, and many questions, but you are already past this place and upon your way again.

After the riding, after you reach the land you long for, there is only memory, shards of vision gathered on your rapid ride, riddles of fleeting sights and songs. These last lines move through the horses's mane and about you before your journey ends.

On the way, we saw her:
Spirited, gleaming mane, trailing tail;
Galloping hard, with grace upon the green plain.
On her back she bore tradition, a child, a fate.
Ranging far, fleet of foot along her journey.
The way, the track of this traveler is the more noble.
Can you guess her name?

THE GIFT

The Rune of Motion calls our attention to a physical mode of travel; the horse. To be sure, this is no ordinary animal. The myths of Britain tell of women who are themselves horses, embodiments of the nobility of the land. In such ancient lore, foals are often associated with the inheriting of kingdoms, with noble children, and with the getting or losing of a fate. There is no better emblem of sovereignty than this creature, for the newborn foal can rise up and use its legs on its first day of life.

This Rune also speaks of harmonious relationships such as those existing between horse and rider, between king and queen, between loving partners, between ourselves and the land, between our minds and our bodies. The saddle is a place of privilege and perspective, a vantage point from which many sights are seen in relation to each other. Yet, like the ancient mounds of the land, such perspective may produce both blows and wonders, both blessings and difficulties.

Yet, sometimes Faery is not the destination itself but is a place you move through, or travel across. It is the best of mythic routes across the Otherworld, where lights shine and flicker, where the waters move swiftly beneath us, where we cross, borne on the back of vision. It is those moments of prescience and perspective we find between the common events of our lives.

Right living ties us to the land and there are aspects of the Horse Rune that speak to such relationships. There yet exists an ancient bronze statue of Epona, the Romano-Celtic horse goddess, that depicts this deity seated with wheat in her lap, and a dish with wheat in her right hand. This dish is held above a horse. Remember the charm? "Hattock" is the old word for a sheaf of wheat. Such knowledge of foodstuffs allows us "free" travel, by making us able to use the bounty inherent in our surrounding landscapes.

In England's West Country, upon just such a fertile landscape, an ancient image of the horse is carved in the surface of the chalk downs. These rolling hills were horse country and symbols of the horses themselves. That land also stands between many ancient kingdoms and so serves as a kind of boundary place, a land between, where the wind does not cease so long as riders ride and horses canter out their traveling songs between the worlds. Only there, astride the wild rolling land, do we untether fortune's steeds and gallop madly towards the faraway.

This Rune's gift is not the wisdom of a single narrative, but of a progression of images, sounds and impressions. Its power lies in the idea of succession and in our ability to build stories from such shards. This Rune and its guardian stand for the wisdom garnered through swiftness, transition, and right travel. It also embodies the vehicles for such journeys; our physical bodies and our imaginative minds.

This charm is a calling for a journey of intention, for traveling between the worlds. Draw this Rune upon the earth in chalk while calling the charm. Speak the name of where you would go and hold on to your hat!

A RUNE OF INSPIRATION

THE CHARM

Fire of invention
canticle of craft
light of poets
friend of fools
child of the cauldron
crown of insight
draught of skill
spark of utterance
breath of genius
awen of wonder:
Awaken and lend
your light.

THE TELLING
The brightest blaze begins with but a little spark, and even a fool may bring a great light into the world.

Before I found him, he kept the fire for another. I do not know how he came to serve as the houseboy of a goddess, or where he was born the first time. But he tended hearth for her, made sure the fire did not become too great nor go out altogether. For a year and a day he watched the flames and kept her cauldron. Now, the cauldron's brew was brilliance, but that gift was not for him. This spell was set cooking for the foolish son of the cauldron's mighty dame. So as servant, the lowly lad watched, and he waited, and added sticks to the fire, or green leaves as they were needed. For all that long year and one day more, the cauldron bubbled, but on the last day of its brewing, the boy fell asleep by the hob, and the brew boiled over. Three burning drops of the sacred stew flew from the cauldron and landed on his thumb. Well, this woke him up, and feeling the pain upon his finger, he thrust it straight away into his mouth.

Now all is changed.

In that instant, he sees the world with new eyes. The world within becomes the world without. The slightest movement of his hand leaves behind a trail of light. And all the portions of the land sing out to him, and in his heart he knows the secret name of every creature, tree, and stone. In that same second, he perceives the fury of the cauldron's owner, feels her anger scorch the ground. He knows that she knows what he knows, and with his wonderment, fear comes flying to his side. He turns to flee, feels his feet stop and then leap away from the ground, his body conforming to his need. He is a rabbit racing from that place, but she changes, too, and soon a greyhound's teeth are inches from his legs. Quick as thought, he is a salmon leaping for the river. She is sleek and dark within an otter's hide, sliding into the water closer, closer, coming fast. He turns upon his fins and leaps high, becomes a bird rising from the current, a swift small bird making for the hedge. Her fur turns to feathers, too. Her paws are wings and claws, smooth surfaced, sharp taloned. Now a hawk, she flies straight up, then stoops for him, as quick as light. He wants to be small, he wants to hide away, to fall into a hole. He holds his breath and becomes a piece of golden wheat, sifting through the grass down to the soil. She pauses, and liking better what another bird might do, shifts one last time into a hen, and, hungry for her due, swallows the wheat-boy down. The rest, for him, is darkness.

As she resumes her natural form, her anger is still great, but now abides and turns in upon itself. He waits within her, growing fast, and well before one summer turns to see another he is born from his new mother. In all those months her fury has not abated, but when she sees the boy, his shining face, his laughing eyes, she cannot harm him by her own hands. Instead she sets

the boy adrift upon the sea, letting fate decide what future will be his. The waves become his cradle, and he learns to love the evening lights, greater and lesser. The sun and moon are father and mother to him in their turns, while all the little lights become his sisters and brothers; the stars, and the dancing flames playing catch-as-catch-can about the prow of his coracle.

He drifted towards land and floated into a weir on May Day. It was there I found him and, pulling back the blanket, said, "Now here's a radiant brow!"

"Yes," the child said, though only three days old, "that shall be my name."

THE GIFT

This Rune embodies the wisdom of artistry and the visions that may be found within the cauldron of inspiration. In Irish, this power is called the *imbras forosnai*, the great knowledge, poetic talent, inspiration that illuminates. In Welsh, it is the *awen*, the fire of poetic insight. You do not open your eyes to see the wonder lights of *awen*: you close them.

In many ancient tales, poetic skill and power manifests itself in the art of transformation, the ability to see the world through the eyes of other living beings. Like the goddess in the telling, certain folk have tried to keep such gifts for themselves, secrets hidden away from the rest of the world. But inspiration is a slippery fish and is not easily held in a single hand.

So, too, this guardian may assume many forms, shifting like a flame, and attending the lives of those it deems worthy. The minds of artists—writers, painters, poets—are its most frequent habitations, but if it is not cared for with respect, or if it is taken for granted, it quickly departs to enlighten the lives of others.

Without inspiration, we fall prey to the other aspect of this Rune; the lights of distraction. This Elf-fire has many names, but is most commonly called Will o' the Wisp, or Jack o' Lanthorn. These are the phantom lights that appear to night travelers, leading them astray into bogs, off the road, out of the way. It is also know as *ignis fatuus*, or foolish fire, for without inspiration, we are fools indeed.

Draw this Rune in colorful inks, or trace it in the air with a bright candle when you seek the fire of vision, or would breathe in the breath of prophecy, or any time your muse has fled and left you in the dark.

63

A RUNE OF ELOQUENCE

THE CHARM

Nine worlds hang about my branches,
well of wisdom winding in my roots.
Every leaf a letter,
each branch an angled rune,
all good tellings fall from my heights,
all good tidings grow from my seeds.
I stand in the heartwood
at the center of every story.
Ash is my name.

THE TELLING

The search for letters and language will require the opening of a faery gate, for all tongues have their origin in the ground, in the land of roots and caverns, in earthlight and the ancient script of stone. When you have traveled far and over many roads, beyond the forests of elm and ash, under the hill and beyond the hall, you may find yourself beside a ruined arch.

Would you seek for wisdom still?

There you may meet a peddler. Perhaps you can see him now, gesturing towards you, his wares rattling in his hands. He smiles wryly, one eye always hidden from view, and points proudly at his treasures. From the runes that spill from his hands and spring up like plumes from his hat, you may guess that he is a keeper of letters, a broker of poetry, a collector of chanting tongues. Languages, signs, and runes are his business. You'll find him still a merry fellow who is known by a hundred names, though many think him somewhat grim and dark

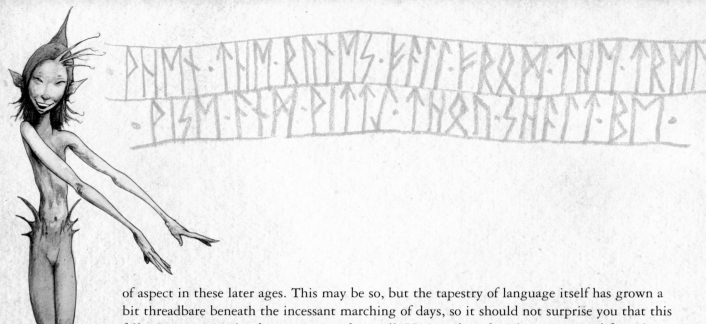

of aspect in these later ages. This may be so, but the tapestry of language itself has grown a bit threadbare beneath the incessant marching of days, so it should not surprise you that this fellow's reputation has become tattered as well. He is endowed with a precise and formal tongue, though his manner of speech is familiar and becomes more so, shaping itself to your ear more and more with each word he speaks.

Would you seek for wisdom still?

If the light is right, the sun slanting low behind the arch, he will reach into his cask and gift you with a letter. One Rune, no more. No other is needed, for from this rune, all other tellings form. His gift to you is the first sound, the *ur*-letter. This Rune is a tree with many branches. Its sound reaches into many songs. Its story is the story of the birth of story.

If you are pleased with this gift, give him your sign of acceptance—a wink. He likes a good story (well, who doesn't?) and loves his own best of all. If you attend him, just now, the tale of the birth of language will be yours to do with as you please.

"In the long and long ago, a time of kings and kennings, of queens and quests, of wordsmiths and wise-women, the world walked its days around a single tree. This tree grew at the very center of the land. In truth, there have been many such trees at many times and in many lands, but all that matters is this; from this first tree came the getting of my knowledge and the nature of my trade. Sigils hung down from its branches and letters formed upon its leaves. Its twigs could be fashioned into words and letters and carried as talismans, or alphabets, or staves of portent and prophecy. But such knowledge does not come without a price and here is how I paid my dues...

"Always, I have been a traveling man, never long for one land, always on my way to another. At this time I had traveled very far on roads I will not name. Much is lost to my mind of those days, but I was upon a quest, this you may be sure, and when I woke one night, I found myself high among the boughs of a great tree. Crows and nightbirds taunted me. Winds blasted the branches and my body.

"Now, the nights were long in those days, so I waited, knowing no good thing can come without a sacrifice: so there I was, given, myself to myself. Nine long nights I adorned the boughs. Great pain attended me but that was the price of knowledge. I had no food, no drink. Nine nights it took until I began to see. I looked only upon the ground. I cried aloud. Something moved about the roots. I reached down and caught the runes up into my hands while spirits moved about the tree before dawn.

"And at last I fell, clutching the runes in my hands. It was then I learned the ancient lore, turning each letter over with my fingers: I knew the allure of language and all secrets became known to me. My wisdom grew, my mind became the waxing moon. Each word opened to another word, another world. Verses grew like seeds where I sought them. Little more can I tell you, but this you must not forget: all language, all books, all songs and tellings begin with but a single letter. One rune to open many doors. *Ur*-words are emblems of power and portent. They breed well. They still hold the smell of the soil. From them, other tellings grow. Here, in this single sign, is the origin of every worthy song and the signature of the father of stories."

Would you seek for wisdom still?

THE GIFT

The guardian of this gate, is known by many names. If you guess one, he may unlock the word-hoard and offer you a letter. From its shape and sound, a story may be told, a song sung, a poem uttered. Or the shape of the offered rune may inspire your shaping hands. In any case, something must always be made from the gift of faery letters. They are the beginning of all noble utterances. Any word spoken well is a sacred thing and is itself an offering to the guardian of this land.

This Rune is the gate to the time of all *ur*-words and the place where early songs were forged and tempered. This is a land most worthy of travel. You will find every glade to be a place of epic, every river ford a bridge to a land and legend yet unknown. If you build fine maps of words within your mind, the power of poetry and place will be known to you. Well, the words themselves are travelers too, shaped by passing through a succession of lands and peoples, each one bearing the signature of its path.

So we are bound to language, tied to the world by the tellings of our tongues. Our words shape, conjure, contain, and constrain the lands around us. This Rune calls upon us to be attentive to language and its creative uses. Here, in the few letters of our alphabets, are the origins of every story that has ever or will ever be told.

Draw runes and letters upon paper, or cut them upon branches and choose them at random to see what words may be formed. Activities such as this, where we play with language and signs, are the birth of story and prophecy. Draw this Rune upon blank paper, or canvas, or any surface that will in time hold a story of your own devising. Look for a single tree (ash is always best, but any will do), standing alone upon the land. Chant the charm and find your door among its roots and branches.

You stand now looking about you, at all the minute creations waiting to be sung into being. Describe them, spell them, conjure them with words and make them known. Call them down from the branches with the letters you have won from the world. Chronicle the winding winds. Paint the triple faces of the moon's three names. Just now, these things are as if they had never been; use the runes and give them life.

A RUNE OF THORN

THE CHARM

We are children of the briar,
uninvited guests
the knots untied
bright cords cut.
We cannot be forgotten
will not fall away
but wait in stillness
at the heart of the hedge.

THE TELLING
The music came to her at night and called her to the greenwood.

Through the gate with stolen key, away from her father's land, and far into the forest she walked until she came to a clearing where night birds sang and their songs hung like jewels upon the boughs and branches. In that glade a pale knight stood, moon upon his shoulder, bold as you please, waiting for the maid with love in his aspect and in his eyes. Many nights he had ridden out of Elfland. Many nights he had sung below her father's castle wall, hoping she would come. Now deep in the wood they danced, and the stars were candles lighting their bower-in-the-green. Before dawn she was safe again within her father's hall, though she could not recall her journey home.

The next evening she waited for his song, but no knight of shadows made music beneath her window that night, nor any other. Now you will think this elven knight untrue. Not so.

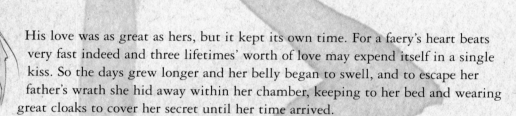

His love was as great as hers, but it kept its own time. For a faery's heart beats very fast indeed and three lifetimes' worth of love may expend itself in a single kiss. So the days grew longer and her belly began to swell, and to escape her father's wrath she hid away within her chamber, keeping to her bed and wearing great cloaks to cover her secret until her time arrived.

When she could hide her state no longer, she stole again into the greenwood and leaning her back against a thorn tree, she gave birth to twin girls. Then her heart was torn in two, for to return with the babes would bring shame to her house, and violence from her father's hands. So she left the children beneath the thorn and called out three times to her lover's kin to care for them. When the girl left the glade, tears hot upon her face, the People of the Forest did come. They took up the children from beneath the thorn tree and carried them far into the woods and kept them as their very own.

She returned to her father's hall. Her heart—nearly broken—grew cold. Years piled up around her feet like leaves in autumn, and briars grew about the walls of her tower. Her life became a quiet round of sleep and waking, each day much like the others until one November's eve, when she awoke in the dark and heard music. Running to the top of the castle wall, she saw the People of the Forest dancing and in their midst, two girls bright of eye and light of step, leaping and turning on the green. Now, she knew them in an instant as her own and called to them with words both sweet and sad, but they did not hear her. Of course they could not, for as close as they appeared to be, they had passed beyond the gate of mist and were no longer of this land. At last the music faded and the girl's heart broke completely. She left her last breath caught within the briars growing up about her father's castle wall.

Now she needs no key to leave and she flies from that place beyond the gate of mist on paths well known to her, over the damp earth to the forest where lights move about the trees. There she joins her daughters in their dance and holds them in her arms, and so at last is healed of her wounds.

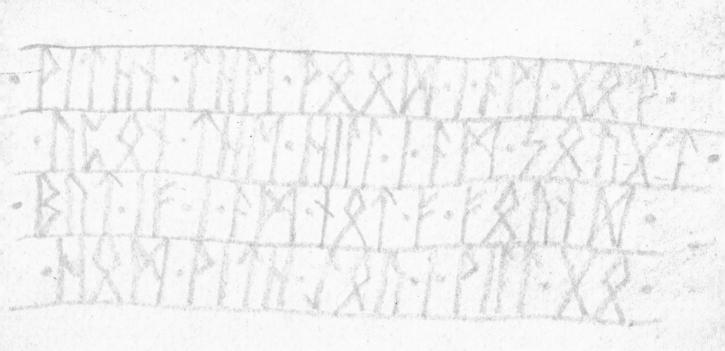

THE GIFT

Though generally never spoken aloud, a single elvish word exists that may indicate any one of three things simultaneously; an accident, a thorn, or a hammer. And while they seem unrelated, when read together, see how they are all part of the same idea. Indeed, the smallest unconscious action may bring a hurt that is hard and terrible indeed.

This guardian's provinces are the bowers of thorn which stand in the Western Isles of Elfland. Hawthorn and blackthorn grow thick upon those islands, for they are places long associated, like the trees themselves, with justice and trial, repentance and punishment. Their shores are reminders that every thorn, every wound may be a test of strength, endurance, and patience, taking the measure of our worth. Her presence, or the drawing of this Rune, must be taken as a warning: chaos is present and the creative powers at play may have dire consequences.

The Rune of Thorn is related to the blast, or faery bolt, sometimes called elfshot. This weapon is used by the elves to punish people for broken social laws, transgressions, and violations of hospitality. Thus this Rune's power is ambiguous. It may be used to make something halt, cease, or stand still, and so is often at the hand of faery healers, whose powers are most efficacious when used to staunch the flow of blood. It is also called the Goblin Rune, for all things dark and destructive have at their heart a single wound, an unhealed moment, an agitation, an act of chaos. Such moments, when brought out into the light of day—like the little thorn—are often seen to be small matter indeed. Yet it is the small, unattended wound that grows worse with time, and the accidental offense left unresolved that festers to sicken our relationships with places, with the sacred, and with each other.

Speak this charm with caution when a hurtful secret must be kept, or when you are caught within the briar and must be still for a time, waiting for a wound to heal.

A RUNE OF JOY

THE CHARM

The living moment
is the place of joy:
fleeting shadow's promise
lightning flash
bursting bud
flowering fragrance
raven's brief delight
hall of feasting
glad laughter
and the closed door of memory.

THE TELLING A king must be a bridge.

There once was a king who lost his head in the Otherworld. But, mind you, it was not truly lost. He made a gift of it to his people, asking them to sever it from his shoulders and to carry it home with them to their own land. The head told them many things: that the road of the company would be long; that it would be many years before they again were home; that they would, during that time, feast gladly despite the melancholy history that lay behind them. They were told that they would come to a hall with three doors, which was to be the chief place of their merriment. While they feasted, the head would not decay and the birds of Rhiannon would attend the company, making music of the Otherworld. And this final fate did the head lay upon them; that if they ever opened the third of the hall's three doors, all the memories of their past would come swiftly upon them and they must then depart that place for home and bury the head at once.

So it was—for a time—that the Company of the Head was a joyous company indeed, and the head was as fine a companion as ever it had been when it rested upon the king's shoulders. But the fate came to be as the king foretold. The third door was eventually opened and melancholy washed like waves over the company. Memories sat in their stomachs like stones as they carried the head swiftly homeward. The head was buried upon the White Hill, and this act was called one of the "three happy concealments." But years later another king removed it, and this was called one of the "three unfortunate disclosures," for while the head lay within the hill, no plague ever came to that land; but after its removal, plague and invasion attended the history of that place like crows about a copse. Such are the spoils of memory's abuse, as the bards relate. But the advice of that first ancient king who lost his head may yet be heeded and the door to the dire past may be closed again. The brimming cup is yet upon the table and the birds of paradise await your glad return.

THE GIFT

The Rune of Joy is found in the instant; in the laughter of friends, in the moment of mirth, in the turn of a dance, and the raising of the full glass. In such moments, a door to Elfland is open to you.

This story and the glad image of the laughing head beg us to ask ourselves: What are the memories we carry that keep us from joy? How can we make a bridge of merriment to carry us beyond painful memories and into the dance that circles ever around us?

How often do we return to painful memories in the cabinets of our minds? How often do we open such doors, only to find ancient disappointments waiting for us? When will we learn to leave such doors shut, and instead look about the landscapes of our present lives for diversion? The opening of doors is always an act of the will. We always have a choice.

An ancient adage tells us: "That the birds of discontent fly about your head, this is unavoidable, but that they make a nest in your hair, this may be prevented." The use of joyful moments, when we are relieved of our obligations to the past, can help heal our minds and bodies. Where we come together in glad company, where there is song and dance, there is the door to Faery and the path of restoration.

Make this mark in spilled wine, or good ale, or sparkling water upon a table or any place of gathering to encourage festivity, mirth, and brimming laughter.

A RUNE OF FATE

THE CHARM

*Above our heads
they are weaving.
Soft voices
across the warp and weft,
careful spinners,
spindle maids,
little sisters,
Habetrot.
Draw out your skein for me.*

THE TELLING *Work, work, for a single hand will but little work command . . . .*

We see her husband leave the house, hear her crying, feel her despair. She must spin one hundred hanks of thread before he returns tomorrow. But she is no spinner. Not in her nature. Not everyone can, you know, for it takes a special hand to twist and measure and cut a skein just so. She is young, yes, and pretty, and so sad now it hurts to see her. So we sing to her from under stone. We sing our little walking song. Of course she hears it, everyone hears it, and then they find us, don't they?

Out she comes into the night, following our little song. She walks one way, then another, follows a stream, and finds a rock upon the hill. She lifts that rock. Sturdy arms. Strong back. Brave girl. Below she finds our cave, each of us sitting on a self-bored stone, and in she comes, bold as blood. In the earthlight she sees us spinning, spinning, spinning, and she

asks us for help. She asks us to help her! Very wise, *very* wise, very *wise*. Of course we will! We tell her she must have us over, for we are neighbors after all. Have us over! What should we bring? Of course we'll come. We'll set him straight, that man of yours. Men are easy. Tomorrow night it is. Wait for us.

The next night, her husband comes home and the house is in a fury. Table set. Candles lit. Wine. All for us? How grand! So busy is everyone at their tasks, he quite forgets to ask about the thread, and before he can remember to inquire after her spinning, company is announced. We wear our green gowns and look very fine, *very* fine, very *fine* indeed. Her man is most polite and invites us all in, and off we go to supper. Oh! The food! Salty tidbits. Sweet trifles. Dainty delicacies. Little morsels of savory meat. Very pretty. But all cooked. Ah, well. All through the meal he looks at us, then looks away, but each time his eyes dart back, drawn like little flies. Finally he asks. We knew he would. He says to us, with all charity, "Ladies, I mean no rudeness, but may I ask how all your mouths came to be turned so…curiously…to one side?" Oh! Such an easy question, so simple an answer. "It's the spin, spin, spinning!" we laugh, with all our lips leering away to the left. "Even the prettiest mouth on the prettiest maid will take a twist to it from pull, pull, pulling out the thread!"

And that was all that needed to be said. That man of hers, he never mentions spindles again; and the girl still comes to the hill and we spin for her instead, for she never could get the talent of it. So she lived happily with her husband then, and a good long life that girl got in the bargain, for so lovely a thread as hers we hate to cut too soon. Three daughters they had, and none of them could spin either, nor were they ever asked to.

THE GIFT

Everyone knows that faery women are famous for their spinning and weaving. Their own looms are very fine, but they seem to prefer borrowing the looms of mortals, a reminder of their fondness for helping and meddling in the fates and affairs of common folk. Just above such stories lurk the Fates themselves and the spiders who are their children. They are the world's first weavers, the creatures who spin and catch, and bind, and help or cut loose a life. When a spider appears in legends and myths, often it is in the role of grandmother. In the old tales, it is the young who meet the Fates or the Spider Grandmother, or the old Habetrot on their road, for they need her wisdom the most. She will work hard to help them, for a lost child is a lost fate, a door closed forever.

The faery Fates—for this is their Rune especially—reside in the very center of Elfland, where they may usually be found weaving the Tapestry of Inheritance. Of course, fate is in part determined by the ancestral past, but it is also tightly tied to your own cleverness. What you get from the world may be a gift or a burden, but what you do with your inheritance, the manner in which you weave it into the tapestry of your life, is entirely up to you.

To cut the strands that bind us to a hard fate, we must withdraw from the momentary and attempt to view the larger tapestry of our lives. We must not only see ourselves as part of the wide-spanning web, but see also the branches that support the web, the trees that raise the branches, the soil that holds the tree, the land that bears the soil, the sea that cradles the land, and the infinite, shining constellations that reflect all the intersecting patterns around us.

The Shears of Fate can cut both ways, for they also sever life when our thread is at an end. But look here, at the faery spider's knowing grin. Perhaps there shall come a moment, bright and new like a sun, when you realize that no fate binds you to the future, that you can ask for help upon your path, that your days and years are your own. At that moment, these guardians cut you free from the web to wander the world as you will.

79

A RUNE OF ARRIVAL

THE CHARM

Falias, Gorias, Findias, Murias.
Behind us
citadel's surety
bright foam upon dark sea
familiar names
and a good death
at the end of days.
Before us
earth-home
green sward
and short-lived victories
sated ravens
and radiant retreat
into earth gods
into fastness
of stone and tree and shadow.

THE TELLING
Falias, Gorias, Findias, Murias.

Follow the root path if you would meet the Ever-Living of Elfland. They are still here, but well hidden. Once great warriors and gods, they have grown distant in the memory, hiding themselves away in the old songs and deep places under stone.

They were great masters of magic, gods and not-gods, for they do not die as we do but keep a radiance and youth about them that does not fade with the passage of time. Their artisans were unmatched, fashioners of splendor. Swords did not blunt, spear shafts warp, nor armor yield. Their harps and harpers were the wonders of the wide world, and even a single note may still conjure all the hues of twilight. Their music weaves together all remembrance: valor, tragedy, birdsong, moonlight on the dark strand, the longings of every age. And though I have heard their harpers play many times, at feast, at revel, and even from within the mounds themselves, never a note can I keep in memory. That is a strange, sad thing and this is the first I have spoken of it.

They are poets of great eloquence and many tongues are known to them. Bird knowledge is their especial gift, and they brought that wisdom to these shores. They taught us what might be divined from the raven's varied calls. If the arrival of warrior guests or poet satirists is imminent, "*grak, grak,*" the bird will say. If women are coming, the call is long. Should a raven be heard from the northeast side of the house, thieves are stealing the horses. If its voice is small, whispering, "*er, er,*" sickness will fall upon some member of the household. If they sing, "*carna, carna, grob, grob, coin, coin,*" wolves are coming. A raven that speaks from a high tree foretells the death of a young lord or knight.

Once proud upon the plain of combat, their names are now the names of hollow places. They attend the earthlight and have become hill folk, the children of the mounds, a hidden people. Though many tales are yet told of their battles and some words are yet whispered of their retreat into twilight, little is known of their origins. On this obscure and distant matter they will speak only four words, "*Falias, Gorias, Findias, Murias,*" and these are spoken with such sadness that the unguarded heart will surely break at the sound of them. These are the names of the cities whence they came. Some folk may speculate further, but more than this is hearsay. Some say the four cities are in the north, some say in Greece. The ravens will give you as likely an answer as anyone else.

I remember their arrival was attended by wonders. They came on the eve of May in a shroud of air and light, a strange mist on the dark sea. Upon their landing, they looked back over their shoulders towards the water and began to weep. They were very tall and resplendent, golden-haired and bright-eyed, and it seemed that even the waves' crashing to shore grew quiet while these folk mourned the world behind them. For three days they stood upon the strand and for three days the sun was lost to us. When true night fell on the third day, they set fire to their ships. It was then I knew they would never leave this land.

THE GIFT

In Ireland, the *Tuatha De Danaan* were once a mighty invading force from across the sea. They overthrew the Fomorians, but were later forced to retreat themselves before the Milesians. When the *Tuatha De* fell before the sons of Mil, they went into the hills of Ireland and became the gods of that place, installing themselves in the memory of the land itself. As Christianity gained a footing in Ireland, their power was diminished again, so they remained a hidden people, smaller than they once were, but still a folk strong in magic wherever their names are honored.

This Rune signifies "otherness" in its most sacred aspects; the exchange of knowledge and the artistic and cultural transformation that are the result of those encounters. It symbolizes the foreign god, invader, or visitor that over time becomes an inner guardian of the land in which it arrives. A slow process, but one suggesting that we may, over many generations, ally ourselves with the spirit of any landscape to which we dedicate ourselves and our children.

The guardian of this Rune is present whenever we encounter the alien, or the foreign becomes familiar, or we widen our cultural horizons. At such times and places, a door to Faery may be found. Rarely should the Rune be used, but drawn only as an act of dedication when you work to ally yourself with lands, people, or ideas that are new and unfamiliar.

A RUNE OF SUSTENANCE

THE CHARM

On the chanting waters run.
Dark course flows, and bright wave
and the branch of blessing borne by flood.
Here brims Milk of Fosterage
Wine of Nobility
Drink of Oblivion.
All things root-wise and stone-sure
  begin to rise
at the call of her spilling names:
Argante, Sirona, Nantosuelta, Coventina,
Boand, Bride, Senna, Frideswide,
Clota, Sequana, Brigantia, Matrona.
On and on the waters run.

THE TELLING
Once a goddess, then a saint, now a frog. Every place of water has a name and a guardian, though their forms may change over time. The guardians of the fords and waterways of Elfland are various and changing, but never insignificant.

Walking out from the city of Oxford, I followed first a road, then a street and a lane, finally a footpath. Always away from town and towards the country. I remember the path lined with elm trees, their leaves grown gold in the early fall, and a small gate leading into a medieval churchyard. Even now, large yew trees may be found there casting long shadows about the gravestones, their roots reaching down into the moist soil. Between the trees and stones there is a well dedicated to Saint Margaret. A few small steps lead down to the rock-lined shaft and above them, on the greening bricks, yellow flowers are often placed as offerings. Somewhere along the dark wall inside the well, a little frog sat, watching me as I watched it. I waited for many moments, hearing only the sound of water stirred by the frog as it began to swim in

circles below me. I reached down, drawing cold water into my hands, then touched wet fingers to my face and eyes. Only then did I hear the Voices of the Wells.

In the well's song, I sensed many rich strains, the chants of dark channels coursing beneath the stretch of soil. She told me of the time when every well and spring of the land had a faery woman who guarded and attended it, offering sustenance to all who came seeking her blessing.

Argante, Sirona

The waters were wide in those days and rivers and springs flowed forth out of Elfland like wine at a feast. At the wells and water places of the land, anyone who came seeking comfort was kindly attended and greeted richly. Fair welcome was for the asking and the wells became places of joy and plenty for wayfarers.

Nantosuelta, Coventina

So in the land of Logres (and all other lands then known), every well had its guardian and each guardian bore a sacred cup and held it dear. From the lips of their cups poured plenty. In the depths of their cauldrons all wondrous sustenance was stirred. From their hands flowed healing without cease.

Boand, Bride

And the rivers had their faery guardians, too, and all places where waters gushed from the living earth were known to pilgrims as sanctuary. About the headwaters were built temples which became the homes of healing and the habitats of prophecy.

Senna, Frideswide

But prophecy cannot be compelled, nor may a hurt be healed by force. Hospitality is a holy gift and may not be grabbed. These are simple truths, as any child knows. Yes, even the infant and her mother sense, by instinct, the protocols of fed and fountain.

Clota, Sequana

Yet there have always been those who hold hospitality cheap. A king came to the land of Logres. His sacred role as protector of the wells he laid aside, by choice. He was the first to break the custom. He enforced a guardian of the wells against her will and carried off her cup of gold. An age of ignorance arose and many followed this king's foolish course. So it came to be that the sanctity of the waters was abused and forgotten. From these sacrilegious acts flowed much sorrow, for not long after the kingdom turned to loss, and the land died and turned to desert. Where fountains flowed, there turned twisting ropes of sand. The forests fell fallow and barrenness attended every house. Not a hazelnut could be found, for folk had lost the Voices of the Wells and the damsels that dwelled within them. All the land was waste and these doors to Faery were closed for a while.

Brigantia, Matrona

The water tracks to Elfland may yet be opened. Much time has passed, but if their ancient names are called, the waters of the Otherworld may rise to your honest plea. The Voices of the Wells may wake to your words and open again the gates of flood and sustenance.

THE GIFT

The Voices of the Wells are quieter now, but they are not silent. To hear them, we need only remember how to listen and how to see. We must anoint ourselves with the quiet songs of a place to partake in the chorus of the waters. Even the ripples of a frog in the dark can carry a message if we will set expectation aside and drink deeply of the experiences carried in the living waters of the land.

The Rune of Sustenance connects us to the tides of imagination. Every well has its particular gifts, its own ability to inspire and bless. Certain wells were thought to cure sterility, but surely this speaks to sterility of the heart and mind as well as the body. Some sacred springs are said to dry up if sought a second time, and there is helpful wisdom in this warning for us too: we must not always seek the same paths of inspiration. Instead, we should quest for new creative avenues, never becoming too dependent upon a single source of inspiration. Even the deepest wells can dry up if they are tapped too frequently.

So seek this rune's guardian in times of barrenness, when you have wandered long in the wastes. Seek her when drought is upon the land, or upon your heart. Wells and springs are locations of healing and restoration and have always been worshipful landscapes. Her charm calls the ancient names of the goddesses of wells, springs, rivers and lakes; thus, wherever you stand in the presence of water, this acknowledgement will help you wake that water's sacred guardian, for in the deep earth, all waters are sisters of the same blood. Her ancient names reflect tales of quests for grails and cauldrons, for streams and wells, for love and remembrance.

Rivers, lakes, wells and pools are the most common boundary places between Elfland and the Middle World where we reside. Such boundaries are permeable and allow respectful travel between the realms. Yet we must never forget that these frontiers can be dangerous during times when the waters of the world are abused. We must then approach such sites in a spirit of reconciliation and honor. Old gods live long within the roots and water tracks of the land, and must be attended with consideration and care.

The best water tastes of the ground, of deep places of rock removed from the sun. Tasting this lonesome water binds us to the land's hidden heart, to that particular place, enabling us to know something of its song. Yet at any place moving water is heard, we may perceive the Voices of the Wells. Waters course below our streets, inside our homes, flow at every instant within our bodies. Because such living water is always traveling, this rune is tied to fate and to all things that move both towards us and away from us simultaneously. Indeed, our ability to live peaceably upon the land is directly linked to our respect for our wells and waterways. Our communal fate is then utterly dependent on the waters of the world and our recognition of their sanctity.

At a place of living water, make the rune upon a broken piece of pottery and cast it into your reflection. Such small sacrifices are part of our ancestral practice. If you have ever skipped a stone, cast a coin into a well, tied a piece of rag in the branches above a spring, or made a wish at a fountain, you have carried this ancient rite into the present and already know something of the living water's threshold. Cast your gift into the water and speak her names if you would seek the fount of inspiration, the well of wisdom, or the spilling waters of the soul's spring.

A RUNE OF STEWARDSHIP

THE CHARM

Where are the letters on the stone,
the vows of obligation
carved long ago?
Where is the Horse of Sovereignty,
the Keeper of the Hill?
I enter the faery fort alone
and offer up my name.

THE TELLING
Now the years have wandered far and long, and I am weary from the weight of mask and sword. The hill fort has been forgotten. Blackthorn brambles grow up about its ruins, and little of the embankment can now be seen. But I have not abandoned it. Many nights I've risked the thorns and climbed the hill, waiting for you to find us, for a promise is a promise after all.

In my time I had heard the oldest stories of the hill, learned how in the hour of the land's greatest need, the champion could be called there. I'd heard it sung that if you climbed the hill and called him from his sleep, the damp earth would swell, the stars would turn, letters would glisten on the cold stone lit by light of moon, and the champion would answer the ancient call and appear.

So on a night much like this one, I walked towards the hills where the land drops and rises like breath. The night was fair, but the land was sick, ravaged end to end with wars,

and the gates of Elfland were hard to find, for few then living remembered how to seek them out. I traveled far on roads known to only a few, over the hedge and beyond the field, by grove of oak and row of beech, across the river and the ridgeway, coming at last to a hill with a ruined wall about its head.

I climbed its banks and called the charm among the broken walls, and the damp earth swelled, the stars turned, and letters glistened on the cold stone lit by light of moon. I waited. Long into the night I waited, and sometime during the dark hours after midnight, I drifted into sleep as hard as the stone I leaned upon. When I awoke, the shadow from that single stone was falling across my face and a golden sword lay in my lap. So the champion had come, and the challenge had been met, for I kept the sword and keep it still. The old guardian passed back into the hill and now another takes his place upon it. If you come yourself to the ruins, and call the charm, and the damp earth swells, and the stars turn, and your own name glistens on the stone lit by light of moon, what then?

THE GIFT

The old places on the land require guardianship for they are a kind of crossroads between this world and the Other. Ruins, abandoned hill forts, circles of stones, the landscapes where the ancient peoples came together—these are the places we may seek for wisdom in times of upheaval. But such wisdom must come at a price, and this Rune asks, "What will you give to the land?" Not hard to answer: find a place whose story has been forgotten and watch over it like your life.

The champions of Elfland are near to us. This particular guardian bears sword and mask. The sword is an emblem of both violence and valor, but its power is small compared to the mask. Through a mask, we see the world with new eyes. New perspectives are granted to us. The mask consolidates power but obscures identity. And so we must come to trust our ties to the Otherworld and its denizens without asking for too many particulars. In standing by our promise to protect the land, we learn that our right actions make us part of a succession of guardians who watch over the hallowed landscapes all around us. It is our collective deeds as stewards that make us worthy of remembrance, setting the guide-mark, leaving a path for future heroes to follow.

And if you meet this guardian among the ruins by stone or shadow, and if it gifts you with the mask of stewardship and the champion's sword, what then? Will you take up arms for Elfland? Will you defend the sovereignty of this world or the Other? Will you stand for the land? If you accept the faery challenge, approach the guardian respectfully and, lifting its mask, find your own face gazing back at you.

A RUNE OF DOMAIN

THE CHARM

Who is the chalk sign
and the absence of a name?
Who remembers the way
and holds the door
with either hand?
Whose song is threshold
portal
Inworld
earthlight
and the word of welcome?

THE TELLING

The oldest gate to Elfland is still found between a giant's staves, and if you want to find that door, you will have to ask one who has been there, for the elder paths into Faery are nearly forgotten. Of course the giants still know about such places for they made them, though giants are not so great in number as once they were. It's hard to find them now, but they do leave signs of their passing, and such marks on the land are usually hard to miss.

You say you have maps? No doubt. New ones. Very clean. These will never do. For to journey into the giant's country you'll need to follow the old names. Travel by the ancient markers on the land, not by signs along new black roads. The hill is not so far as you might think! Begin at the Ox Crossing, where the little pigs and dragons sleep beneath the town. Go not to Caesar's Camp, but follow the horse track instead. Stop not at the House of Volund, no, not yet, but find the Seven-Beds-For-Seven-Kings, then

go to Great Circle and Mound of the Mother. Then turn your face into the cold and you shall see him surely.

The Door Warden, the Long Man, the Lanky Man, if you like, is a very old giant and still guards his door, but little is known of him, for he is a very private fellow. His image still stands upon the hill, but it's hard to know whether he walks in this world or the Other at any given time. Because of his love of travel, some think he is dead, and you may even have heard a tale or two about that giant's demise, a simple story told by silly folk who know no better. Some say the Long Man tripped over the ridge of the hill and died in the fall. Or that a shepherd threw his dinner at the giant and slew him with stew, if you can believe such a thing. Or that another local giant and the Long Man had a fight and hurled boulders at each other until one struck our friend and laid him low. Such things have been known to happen, but do not believe these stories, for like all giants, the Long Man likes to wander and is wandering still, I have no doubt.

Indeed, he has always been a traveler, wandering out of Elfland in the early days. Yes, he walked out of that hill at midwinter, and thinking the land about looked fine enough, he marked that place with a sign to remember it by (for as you know, a giant's memory is far shorter than his stride). So the Long Man laid down his walking staves and his pack of branches upon the grassy slope. From the pile, he selected the supplest twigs (logs to you and me) and wove them into the semblance of himself and set this figure upright near the barrow that now stands at the crest of the hill. Now this wooden figure stood for some time before the winds and rain wore it down. Long after this, people came to live at the foot of that hill and, dreaming something deeper than the turf, carved a figure into the chalk beneath the grass upon the slopes. And there his portrait remains. A good thing too, for without his picture in the chalk he might have long ago forgotten the way back into Elfland.

If you follow my counsel and find the Long Man still upon his hill, and call in the ancient way, he may open that hill for you and greet you as a friend. He may tell you the secret of his staves, how he moves about them in the manner of the sun. He may tell you or he may not, for that is a very great secret, even among giants. In any event, he will likely give a gift to you, for it's only polite after you've walked so far. Oh, he is quite a gift-giver. You may receive an enormous shoe, or a cow, perhaps a log with pretty bark. Once he gave me a standing stone, which he pulled from a henge circle like a loose tooth, but how I got it home I'll never tell. Or, if you are very lucky, he may present you with a copy of a very ancient book written when the world was young, full of many strange tales. This book you may keep, for here it is.

THE GIFT

When we talk of giants, we invoke the deepest levels of the land—the rocks below the hills, the strata of the storied earth, the massive living poetry of place. Their ancient bones endure beneath us, even now, and are at times revealed by wind, or rain, or story, only requiring our recognition to open the hallowed portals of rock and hill.

Many classical and medieval writers associated giants with the first world, the age of chaos, and spoke of human creation originating in the blood of giants. If this is so, we are bound inexorably to the primordial past, the living magma from which the world was born. So we descend from these strong creatures who proudly walked the bounds of their domain, always living with the feel of native soil beneath their feet.

By their nature, giants belong to the wilderness, avoiding the agricultural fields and cultivated, fertile plains of civilization. The lands on which we find evidence of giants exist where wilderness has not been wholly erased. Because of the close association of giants—both stories of them and their physical remains—with wild country, we watch for such landscapes to indicate the presence of Faery generally. Where we find the wind-blasted tor, and the wildwood, where storms cry out to each other from cairn to cairn, and the stone walls crumble under the weight of years, we are close to the main gate of Elfland.

Just behind the guardian's image, a chalk outline can be seen. Such figures were carved upon some of the hills of Britain as markers and reminders. But by whom and for what purpose is often a mystery, the subject of much speculation and suspicion. Yet, there is great power in such mysteries for regardless of their origins, all chalk figures scrape the surface of the land away, revealing evidence of an inner mystical landscape, always just there, bright beneath the soil.

Behind every story worth telling, there is a hidden portion of the giant's song. This singular, monumental ballad is called in its entirety "The Great Lay of *Ur*-land," and is the longest and best-known epic in Elfland. It is extremely old, even by elvish standards, and recounts the creation of every tump and stone once within the giant's domain. At one time, if you spread the song out along the ground, it would have corresponded—hill for hill and tor for tor—with the topography of the living earth. But the days of old are long behind us, and the land is not as it once was. Many of the wondrous monuments once known to giants have now vanished from the earth, mined into oblivion, torn up, worn down. But the memory of such sites lives on within the stone-vaulted chapters of the lay itself. Beyond the *Ur*-gate of Elfland, all the lost and ancient landscapes are still preserved in song. If they are found and remembered, you may sing them back into the waking world again.

A RUNE OF PRESERVATION

THE CHARM

River bark
stag bells
sharp wind
water become bone.

THE TELLING
Traveling in winter is a dangerous business yet it is often done for necessity, adventure, or other reasons unknown to sensible folk who keep to their hearth-sides. If you leave your hearth by midwinter moonlight (and I don't recommend it), traveling in the lee of frozen hedgerows and snow-covered badger tracks, over waters held fast in crystal clutches, you will come to her land. Here is a curious kingdom. There is no court, no throne, no halls of ice as you might expect. You will find only two cold stones around a small fire. There you must sit, and if your visit pleases her, she will favor you with a tale. Storytelling is her province after all, and every story ever spoken in winter is known to her.

Listen now.

She speaks of two brothers who set out in bad weather and sought shelter in a ruin where they held the dark night at bay by telling the story of their misadventure. The dark is cold, the weather wild, and, to shorten the long night, one brother tells the other a story much

like their own. The story begins with the words, "Two brothers set out in bad weather and seek shelter in a ruin…". The teller then retires, leaving his tale unfinished. When the fire dies down and both brothers are asleep, Death comes to join them. Only the younger brother survives the night. He escapes death by jumping through his elder brother's unfinished story. So was winter held at bay. Thus stories are still a way to escape death, to travel safe across a dangerous season. However, there is always a price to be paid, she will tell you.

Listen.

Now she sings of ancient kings and queens, held in ice below the ground, their secrets known only to the frozen soil. Her words conjure visions of the rolling hills and the ancient mound-lands. There was a queen, she says, buried with six horses. She will show their bones to you if you ask, and if these relics are scattered upon the snow, patterns of meaning may be discerned between their fallen forms, angles of an ancient language. As she points among the bones, you imagine the outline of the queen's buried frame, still and stately, below the ice. Look closer. See how each bone plays its part, weaves with other forms to frame a vision. Here horses fall about her in the ground and rest their hooves upon her shroud. Here is an offering: the suggestion of a mirror. Clouds move upon that secret face of glass, and beneath them, in reflection, two figures sit about a winter fire, gazing at bones cast upon the ground.

She will tell you that the ancient songs about this queen are all but forgotten now, but perhaps the knowledge of her presence in the land will knock a tale or two loose from your mind. Perhaps you know of something hidden in the earth that requires remembrance. She may show to you other artifacts from the first story of the world—shards, beads, holed stones, or the simple song of seeds, waiting for the warming ground.

So.

She may also whisper of the daring soul who sets out by midwinter moonlight and goes quietly by hedgerow and hidden trackway, wandering far from hearth and home…

If you are pleased with her telling, you should offer her a story in return. Indeed, this is her dearest hope, for every time a story is told in winter her kingdom is conjured and the bounds of her land are extended for a time. I should tell you that this is also your only way to get back home. Only by the gift of a story will your daring winter journey wind you safely back again to your own land.

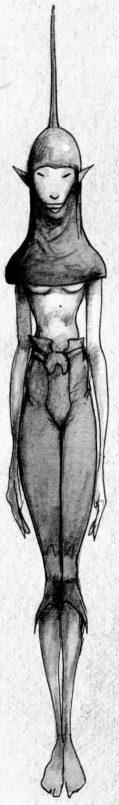

THE GIFT

The Rune of Preservation finds its expression in ice and the frozen land. We often see winter as the season of death and darkness, but this is only an irony of the ice. Protecting snows insure that abundant plants will grow from winter's sleeping seeds. Snowfall and frozen waters open territories and landscapes hidden or inaccessible to us during the green months of the year. During winter, northern people have made windows from sheets of ice, thus gaining visions of a world separate from the safety of their hearths. Turn this Rune on its side and behold a bridge—from one world to another, from winter back to summer, from the frozen wastes to the running waters of our world—this Rune's power lies in preservation and conveyance.

This Rune is a simple line, the earliest mark, and is used to build other letters. This attests to the primacy of winter and the vitality of memories held safely beneath the snow and ice. It shows us something of silence, of preparation, of the waiting time that is the birth of all things. Dark seasons are ancestral and primordial spaces, containing the origins of every elder song and story. Look again at her gown, her crown, her wand: the glint of every frozen drop is a memory, a bright and ancient star to guide your way across the seasons, across the wastes.

All the stories ever told are only pieces of a single mighty epic that began in winter and whose origin is now hidden deep below the snow and ice of Elfland. There is no end to this telling and you are already a part of it, an essential element. Draw this Rune upon the hearth during the deep heart of winter to conjure the voices of the First Ice and to inspire the telling of tales.

A RUNE OF LOSS

THE CHARM

What the flood tide gives as gift
The ebb shall carry from your grasp.
I do not sing in honeyed songs.
My hair is gray with age.
It is no hardship to live below the ground.

THE TELLING

I will speak of stones and the shield-arm grown thin to the bone.
I will talk of hunger and the mother of the spring.
I will sing of the hag who once was queen.
I will tell you of a dream . . .

The bounty of the fields had faded and dark earth looked up at the sky. I walked there upon an early winter morning, over the ancient trackways, past the gaping barrow, beside hills and henges built by the work of hands long still. I rested on the twisting roots of trees, sheltered within the fading mist and fog.

I dreamed her there, among the broken circles of Avebury, gathering twigs and icy leaves

from the base of a humped gray standing stone. She had wandered far from the Highlands, where I had only lately heard she'd roamed about the fallen tower at Dun Ardtreck in Skye, laughing wildly and hurling rocks at the ruined church in the next county. She is various and singular in regard to location, and word of her has come to me from the west of Ireland, from the shattered well on the summit of Ben Cruachan, from the Isle of Man, and from the Lowlands where she has also been known to walk loudly upon the cold nights, there among the stones, busy about her work of making mountains.

The Celts and Romans, Jutes, and Saxons knew of her, though she was wholly ancient by their times. The rocks tell a different story of her travels, but it is difficult to discern upon their weathered faces.

As to what might have coaxed her so far south from the ancient Pictish lay, I cannot say. For she heeds not the words of men in this age and keeps to her own path, often moving beneath the ground on roads no longer known. And indeed, any place of stone may be a home to her.

The Cailleach continued quietly about her work, finding twisty branches and putting them in a basket strapped to her back. Her full and tattered apron, hanging low beneath her waist, was filled with stones and each time she bent to retrieve a twig, a flint or two fell out upon the frozen ground.

Even when standing, she was bent, and dark, and large for one so old. Yet she had a great stride and stepped ably over even the largest boulders. Her face was a carving of spirals, harrowed and blue with aspects of age and winter. As I gazed, I must have moved, for the frozen turf cracked beneath my shifting weight. She turned and, holding me in the moment of her regard, threw a small carved stone at me and laughed hysterically.

I watched her circle the standing stones of the field for many moments in the manner of the Grianan, the winter sun, but when I stood and motioned towards her, her shadow became indiscernible from that of the weathered rock, and I knew she had gone below. The wind resumed, but colder, and I was standing in the shadow of that rock.

THE GIFT

Inherent in The Rune of Loss is the nature of change; the future that comes without concern for the present, the inevitable power of wisdom gained through seeing things as they progress through time. As an avatar of fate, the hag is both sword and sustenance, both winter and spring, both witch and woman: the mother of everything cyclical, everything that turns and changes and goes again to ground. Yet change can be a dangerous business. When we endeavor to change, we walk the parallel paths of creation and destruction because nothing ends without something arriving to take its place. Her nature is that of the hailstone leveling crops, yet changing to water in time, a thing most necessary for future growth. Stories of her travels and travails remind us that abundance is fleeting and must never be taken for granted. Knowledge gained from the observation of cycles is her gift. Discounting our individual and collective roles in history, especially in relation to place, is done at our peril.

In folklore, the hag is always part of the landscape. The mounds and barrows are her body, places of initiation and remembrance. She reminds us of the past of place through the use of stones. Pebbles, flints, and sites formed of stone hold her memories to the ground. Each individual rock has fallen from her apron, from her mind, and from her hand. Such landscapes and artifacts provide an ancient kind of sustenance, a knowledge born of hardship and weathering, reminders of endurance, but also of the inevitability of diminishment over time.

She is everything that is slow to stir but that arrives with great consequence. So we must approach the ancient and inevitable with respect. She is unspeakably old, yet there is telling movement in her form. Her frame is every story lashed together with memory's haggard threads. She is the shield of story and the cauldron of tradition. There, making a slow and striding dance across the peaked and storied land, is there not music in the passing shadow of her hidden name? She holds both a joint of meat and a sword, asking how hungry are you for lost knowledge? Will you strive to remember the voices of the past whatever the cost?

Her realm includes those portions of Elfand most often lost to the modern world; the frontiers of crumbling kingdoms, the plains of forgotten epics, ruins, mead halls, stone circles, barrows, and the landscapes of ancestral memory. She inhabits all places where we forget to ask, "What has happened here?" She pauses at every hearth-side where a story is begun but left unfinished.

To find her forgotten country, seek a place of stone under the waning moon; or cast her rune into a pool of dark water; or call the charm during a hailstorm. Or, better still, ask your grandmother (or her memory, which yet lives within your mind), to tell you of her travels. Ask her to show you the stone she found as a child and keeps in a box under the bed. Ask her of the lands she knew. Ask her about her grandmothers. Ask her to tell you of the moon of her youth. In its light will be your door.

A RUNE OF YEARS

THE CHARM

*Her mantle is bright
in the land of morning,
an arc of hope
for the rising year.
When dark earth holds her,
let no sadness
attend the wake,
only the song of winter
and the whisper of seeds
saying
all the land is alive.*

THE TELLING

Not long ago and across the moor, an old woman kept a garden. Even during the bright noonday sun, she would tend her flowers, working her hands down into the loam to loosen the soil for new bulbs, searching out even the smallest weed. Of the many flowers growing there, the tulips were her special favorites. These were very fine indeed, tall of stalk and bright of petal. So wondrous were these flowers, and so delightful was their arrangement to the eye, that the pixies of the neighborhood became fond of them as well and might be heard, upon the hour of midnight, singing lullabies to their children among the flower beds.

Now it is no small thing for a mortal garden to garner the attention of Elfland, and because the pixies loved these tulips so, they put their hands upon them in a manner of blessing known only to them. From that time forward the tulips grew even brighter than before and acquired a rare and wondrous perfume that would shame lavender and make a rose

bow its head. Each day the garden grew more resplendent. The old woman loved each short-lived bloom like a child of her own, and would never allow even one to be picked. So the pixies kept their brilliant bower and were well pleased with it.

The years passed and when the woman died, other folk came to live in her small house on the far side of the moor. Her tulips were all pulled up, for fools find flowers impractical; and parsley was planted in their place. This pleased the pixies not at all, so they put their hands upon the plants again but with malice at the tip of every finger. No sooner was this done than all the parsley withered to the root, and the plants in all the other beds were dry as bones by morning. But while nothing would grow in that garden, the grave of the old woman became a paradise. Music was often heard about the plot, and it became widely known that the faeries sang dirges and lamentations there on certain nights of the year. Not a single weed grew upon her grave, and it was always green and fragrant. In springtime, tulips raised their heads about the gravestone though none were ever planted there.

THE GIFT

The nature of the Rune of Years is found in all cycles. All things subject to the seasons—plants, people, love, lives, patience—all are watched over by the guardian of this Rune. She teaches that the garden gate to Elfland is found between the furrows, in the patterns of falling fruits, in the spirals and thorns of the berry's briar, in the ritual spacing of the planting beds, and, most sacred of all, in the waiting time before the bloom and harvest. In such patterns and in the in-between places of the verdant world may Faery be found. Some of the oldest stories of Elfland tell of finding it while under the shade of the apple tree or within the orchard or garden. So places where people attend to growing plants—becoming caretakers of the green earth—seem to share a wide frontier with Elfland. Through this Rune we may discern the presence of larger patterns within even the small span of a single flower's life.

The shape of the Rune is not merely the sign of years and harvests but of reciprocity, of one hand giving to another. It is the bounty of labor, the bright fruits that come from attention to the land. Likewise our relationships with Elfland must be cultivated and cared for. We must attend the Otherworld in its changing aspects as it lives and thrives and falls across the calendar. Finding the gate open and rejoicing to feel the rich soil of Faery under our feet and falling through our fingers, remember we are gardeners all.

A RUNE OF EMERGENCE

THE CHARM

Asleep beneath
the bark of evening,
you are young again.
Wake now within
the brightening air,
Messenger of Morning.
Rise and cast off
your coat of stars.

THE TELLING
We have wandered very far together. Over fen and marsh, beyond forest and briar, over the hedge, under the moon, through the fire. We have ridden the white horse across the ridgeway, climbed the hollow hills and journeyed down below them, walked with Winter across the ice to meet the hail's hoary dame, run beyond the garden gate, and circled sun-wise about the stones.

Walk with me one more time.

At the furthest frontier of Elfland an ancient tree grows so high that the stars roost about its branches. To seek it, travel at dusk to the edge of the lands you know. There you will find a forest lost in twilight. Walk to the center of this wood and wait for the setting sun. Watch carefully, for where the sun's beams last alight among the branches, there will be the bower where Day was lost to the world, caught by the goblins and trapped for a time below the bark.

The Day-child was lost. Lost from Night, his mother. Lost from the land. Lost from the light. Dark was the world then, for Night walked long and far over the earth looking for her stolen son. The goblins had taken him: they crept stealthily into the bower of evening, and while she slept they grabbed the babe from between his mother and the wall. Deep within the heart of this tree the Day-child was hidden, crying for his mother to find him. His small tears were jewels, warm beads of amber, and with every drop that rolled off his cheek, a bit of the wood began to soften. His crying reached the ears of the goblins and even their rabid hearts slowed and finally slept, for a child's cries—unbearable to most—are like a lullaby to them.

So the goblins snored and the wood began to bend and the bright boy burst forth from the tree. Day came again into the world and the lamps of dawn were lighted. The heart of Night was eased and she retired to her sphere. And so it goes even now, when Night walks the land, Day sleeps safely in her cloak, high among the branches, but each morning he goes gladly from that tree, flying, laughing, free. And this is the tale of the First Morning of the World that is told each day in the halls of Elfland.

THE GIFT

Every dawn, darkness falls from us and we may, if we choose, revel in the rising of the sun. Each day affords this sacred opportunity; the chance to begin again. The guardian of this rune shows us that the end of one story is always the beginning of another.

The rune of emergence is evidence that creation is a process of cycles, constantly renewing itself. Tradition sings of many lost children, stolen and found. Though locked away in darkness, such youths emerge from their imprisonment strong and capable, ready to aid heroes and kings in the restoration of land and kingdom. These lost children later become great leaders themselves.

When you open this door to Elfland, you stand upon a threshold where the light of the first morning, and this morning, and all the mornings of the world, shine at once. Here is where the sun's road and all the bright paths to Elfland have their origin. Rise before it is light and draw this Rune in the dew on the grass, and find this gate in the fading mists of dawn, even now.

RUNIC ALPHABET

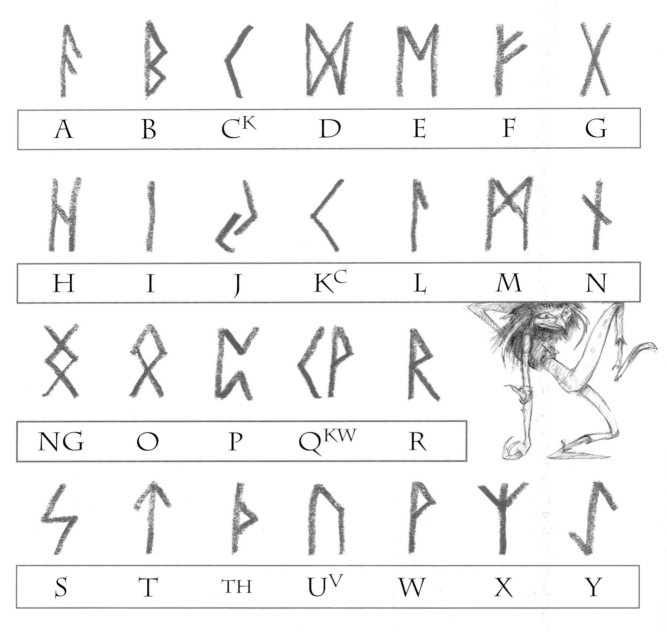

A	B	C^K	D	E	F	G

H	I	J	K^C	L	M	N

NG	O	P	Q^{KW}	R

S	T	TH	U^V	W	X	Y

OTHER POSSIBLE ALTERNATIVES USED
IN RUNIC INSCRIPTIONS

K	O	Y

NOTE: Elvish runic inscriptions are notoriously problematic. Some contain errors, puns or omissions that may annoy mortal sensibilities. Keep your wits about you. Remember, elvish wisdom is never easily won.